The CHOCOLATE Snowman Murders

The
CHOCOLATE
Snowman
Murders

·A Chocoholic Mystery·

JoAnna Carl

AN OBSIDIAN MYSTERY

OBSIDIAN
Published by New American Library, a division of
Penguin Group (USA) Inc., 375 Hudson Street,
New York, New York 10014, USA
Penguin Group (Canada), 90 Eglinton Avenue East, Suite 700, Toronto,
Ontario M4P 2Y3, Canada (a division of Pearson Penguin Canada Inc.)
Penguin Books Ltd., 80 Strand, London WC2R 0RL, England
Penguin Ireland, 25 St. Stephen's Green, Dublin 2,
Ireland (a division of Penguin Books Ltd.)
Penguin Group (Australia), 250 Camberwell Road, Camberwell,
Victoria 3124, Australia (a division of Pearson Australia Group Pty. Ltd.)
Penguin Books India Pvt. Ltd., 11 Community Centre,
Panchsheel Park, New Delhi - 110 017, India
Penguin Group (NZ), 67 Apollo Drive, Rosedale, North Shore 0632,
New Zealand (a division of Pearson New Zealand Ltd.)
Penguin Books (South Africa) (Pty.) Ltd., 24 Sturdee Avenue,
Rosebank, Johannesburg 2196, South Africa

Penguin Books Ltd., Registered Offices:
80 Strand, London WC2R 0RL, England

First published by Obsidian, an imprint of New American Library,
a division of Penguin Group (USA) Inc.

First Printing, October 2008
1 3 5 7 9 10 8 6 4 2

Copyright © Eve K. Sandstrom, 2008
All rights reserved

OBSIDIAN and logo are trademarks of Penguin Group (USA) Inc.

LIBRARY OF CONGRESS CATALOGING-IN-PUBLICATION DATA:

Carl, JoAnna.
The chocolate snowman murders: a chocoholic mystery/JoAnna Carl.
p. cm.
ISBN 978-0-451-22506-1
1. McKinney, Lee (Fictitious character)—Fiction. 2. Chocolate industry—Fiction. 3. Winter
festivals—Fiction. 4. Michigan—Fiction. I. Title.
PS3569.A51977C5 2008
813'.54—dc22   2008006733

Set in Stempel Garamond • Designed by Elke Sigal

Printed in the United States of America

For the Old Broads—

Carolyn, Judy, Marcia, and Merline

Acknowledgments

With many thanks to many people who helped me with information for this book. They include Betsy Peters, who okays the chocolate bits; lawmen Jim Avance, Bob Swartz, and Lieutenant Ralph Mason; Nancy Anderson, gallery director, artist, and art show expert; Ginny Weber, of Jeff's Key and Safe; photographer David Gill; truck owner David Walker; and Susanna Fennema, who keeps an eye on new wrinkles in anthropology. As always, I owe my Michigan neighbors, Susan McDermott, Tracy Paquin, and Dick Trull, big-time. And thanks to Johnny Owens, who with a generous donation to the Lawton Arts for All Campaign bought the right to have his real name used for a fictional character.

Chapter 1

"If you don't want to serve on committees," Maggie McNutt said, "you should stop bringing chocolate to meetings."

"Maybe I could send the chocolate and stay home," I said. "I just don't understand how I get suckered into these things."

"That's easy to explain. First, they ask you way ahead. . . ."

"Yeah, last July."

"Second, someone you really like and want to get along with is sent to make the request."

"Barbara, my banker. She told me she was devastated because she had to step down as treasurer and was desperate to find a replacement who could write a financial report."

"Gotcha! You didn't have a chance." Maggie laughed and downshifted her red VW Beetle as she turned into the long drive that led to the Warner Point Conference Center. "Come on, Lee! Serving on committees is one of the prices we pay for being Americans. I try to think of it selfishly."

"Selfishly? What do you get out of serving on the Winter-Fest committee? I'm in business in this town. A community promotion is supposed to help TenHuis Chocolade make money. But what does a teacher get out of it?"

"WinterFest is an extra opportunity for my students to

strut their stuff. Besides, I can use the work I do now to black-mail other people into helping with my speech and drama fes-tival in April. I use this committee to get what I want. And I want a lot."

Maggie pulled the Beetle into a parking place in front of the conference center's main entrance. I picked up my brief-case and the box of chocolates I'd brought, then popped the buckle of my seat belt. "Ah, Maggie," I said, "you do want a lot, but you mainly want it for your kids."

"That's part of it, Lee. We have talented kids at Warner Pier High School, and also kids who can use these activities to improve their personalities and their lives, or just to have fun. But if the kids do well, I do well. My professional reputa-tion is enhanced."

We both got out of the VW, and we looked at each other over the top of the car. "Now come on, Lee," Maggie said. "TenHuis Chocolade isn't going to go down the tube if the WinterFest flops. So what's your real, true motivation, Ms. Cynical?"

"I guess it's more fun to live in a community where things are happening, so I have to help make 'em happen. Plus, I'm a big girl. I could have told Barbara no. I just like to gripe about it."

"And now that we've established our self-centered credentials . . ."

"Ta-da! It's time for the planning committee for the War-ner Pier Winter Arts Festival! Changing the world! One meeting at a time!"

Maggie began to whistle the Mickey Mouse Club theme song, and I joined in. We did a high five as we fell into step at the front of the Volkswagen, and we kept whistling as we marched through the slushy parking lot and up the steps of the conference center.

The center had begun life as the lavish summer home of

famed defense attorney Clementine Ripley. After she died it wound up as the property of Warner Pier, the prettiest resort town on Lake Michigan. Remodeled to contain a restaurant, banquet and party facilities, meeting rooms, and offices, the collection of limestone buildings was now used year-round. And one of its uses was housing an office and meeting room for the Warner Pier Winter Arts Festival.

Maggie is speech and drama teacher at Warner Pier High School, and I'm business manager for TenHuis Chocolade, which according to the sign in our window produces and sells "Handmade Chocolates in the Dutch Tradition." Maggie and I make an ill-matched pair physically, since I'm a shade under six feet tall, and I inherited light blond hair from the TenHuis side of my family, and Maggie is a shade over five feet and has dark hair and eyes. But we are both emotionally committed to Warner Pier, which we regard as the best of the string of quaint resort towns along the eastern shore of Lake Michigan.

Warner Pier's business community for several years had sponsored a winter trade and tourist promotion. A couple of years earlier, it had been the "Teddy Bear Getaway" in February. This year we were trying a new time frame—Christmas vacation—and our logo featured a snowman.

As we reached the door of the conference center, we each gave a salute to one of the festival mascots, a giant snowman. The WinterFest had financed two seven-foot snowmen, similar to athletic team mascots. Each of them could be worn as a costume so that king-sized snowmen could add atmosphere at each of the cultural events of the festival. When they weren't being worn, one snowman was propped up on Warner Pier's main drag, Peach Street, and the other guarded the entrance of the conference center.

Maggie and I kept up the "Mickey Mouse" racket as we came in the building and waved to Jason Foster, who was doing his manager act in the restaurant to the left of the entrance. Then we marched down a long hall to the office of the Winter Arts Festival—WinterFest for short.

Our levity didn't seem to please the festival's immediate past chair, Mozelle French. As we entered she looked at us sharply over the top of her reading glasses. My private nickname for Mozelle is "Civic Virtue." She takes life a bit too seriously, a trait I find annoying. So, just to annoy her further, I quit whistling and started singing, still to the tune of the theme song of the children's TV show.

"W-I-N! T-E-R! F-E-S! Ti! Val!"

Maggie started singing, too. "WinterFest! WinterFest! Together let us hold i-cic-les high! High! High! High!" Then we whistled the chorus again, ending by banging down our paperwork. The office was furnished with castoffs, so my briefcase and Maggie's file folder were not going to scar the rickety table. I put the box of chocolates down more gently.

"I'm glad to see that you two are enjoying this project," Mozelle said. She didn't mean that. I could tell by her too-virtuous smile.

Mozelle didn't annoy me because she was too good. She annoyed me because she acted too good. According to the local grapevine, Mozelle had grown up in Warner Pier and in her youth had studied art. She still produced anemic watercolors. But twenty-five or thirty years earlier, she had married a dentist and turned into a professional volunteer. Today she was a childless widow and a veteran worker for the Winter Arts Festival, the Autumn Harvest Carnival, the Summer River Gala, and the Spring Home Tour, not to mention the Historical Society, the Study Club, and the Warner Pier Non-Denominational Fellowship Church. I don't know if she was really good at these things, or she just looked as if she ought to be. Her dark hair was always disciplined into a smooth chignon, her weight was right where the doctor recommended, and her makeup never failed to be perfect.

"If we can't enjoy the project, what's the point?" Maggie said. "And I'm happy to report that the play is shaping up very well. Rehearsals are at seven p.m. every evening this week."

Mozelle gestured toward a meek-looking man already seated at the table. "I'm glad someone has some good news. George has lost the juror for the art show." She made it sound as if George had laid the juror down in the wrong place and couldn't remember where he put him.

"That was careless of you, George," I said, "especially since we'd already paid him. Now we'll have to try to get our money back."

"The juror had already selected the show entries from the slides," Mozelle said. "It will be almost impossible to find another qualified person who's willing to work from entries someone else selected."

"What happened to the original juror?" I said.

"He's in the hospital with a broken leg," George said. "It's a bad injury. He'll have to go to rehab. A trip from Washington, D.C., to Michigan is out of the question." Then he spoke directly to Mozelle. "But I didn't finish my story. Dr. Jones has recommended a replacement, and I've already checked the fellow's résumé and talked to him. The new man says he can work from Dr. Jones' preliminary selections, and they'll split the fee. So the problem is already solved."

"Thank goodness!" This news seemed to soothe Mozelle slightly. She sat down near the head of the table, looking a bit less prim, and officiously began to sort through her own papers.

George Jenkins runs a successful art gallery on Peach Street. Like Mozelle, he's active in a lot of community organizations; I know he served on the board of the Holland women's shelter, and he has chaired numerous art shows. George is close to seventy, I'd guess. He always wears classic sweaters and tweed jackets, and his thick white hair is modishly cut. I towered over him, but I towered over nearly everybody on the committee.

Maggie and I shed our winter jackets and sat down at the meeting table. George winked at us, and we both smiled back. All three of us knew what Mozelle's real problem was.

Her problem was that she was immediate past chair, not chair. Mozelle likes to run things. She'd been chair of the WinterFest the year before, and she'd expected to be chair again. But the Warner Pier Foundation—parent organization for the WinterFest—had picked a different person to head the committee. Mozelle hadn't yet recovered from the shock. Even a tactful request from the new chair, asking Mozelle to be the official WinterFest spokesman, hadn't changed her attitude. She acted as if being interviewed on television was an imposition, and she declared herself annoyed by calls from the *Chicago Tribune* and *Detroit Free Press*.

Mozelle could have declined gracefully and left the committee—as past chair she was ex officio anyway—but she seemed to think we'd go astray without her moral guidance.

Besides, the committee did need Mozelle as a spokesman. Our public relations chair, Mary Samson, was terrific with news releases and phone calls, but she was shy. She was not good on television or radio, and she knew it. Mary was happy to do the grunt work and let Mozelle handle the public appearances.

Mary was the next person to arrive. Mary was another Warner Pier native who'd been away and come back. Local gossip was that she couldn't find a job in her chosen field of communications, so she was squatting in the house she'd inherited from her parents until something turned up. Mary always looked as if she'd cut her dark brown hair with garden shears, and that day her sweatshirt seemed to have spaghetti sauce down the front. We all spoke to her, but the greeting she gave back was inaudible.

Then she handed out a sheet headed "Festival Talking Points." It was clear, concise, neat, complete, easy-to-read—everything public relations material should be.

"This is great, Mary," I said.

Mary ducked her head and mumbled. The contrast between her shy, dithery persona and her polished product was astounding.

Amos Hart, who was in charge of the musical aspects of the Artsfest, was the next arrival. He wore a hat with furry earflaps, a long overcoat, and boots that laced. As he shed the layers, his standard indoor attire came into view; Amos was one of the few men in Warner Pier who wore ties, and he was the only one who wore bow ties. Today he had on a red one, contrasting with a white shirt and black suit.

"Hello, all," Amos said. "Lee, we could still use another alto."

"Sorry," I said. "I couldn't learn even 'Rockabye, Baby' in two weeks."

Ever since Amos found out that my alleged talent was singing—back when I was on the Texas beauty pageant circuit—he'd been after me to join one of his choirs. A retired professor of music, he directed two choruses: the Warner Pier WinterFest Chorale and the choir of Warner Pier Non-Denominational Fellowship Church. I didn't have the classical training he needed for the chorale, and I wasn't comfortable with the philosophy of the church, so I had declined. He was good-natured about my refusals, but he kept asking.

Amos was what my college friends and I used to call a "public pray-er." Although he wasn't ordained, he seemed to be down at that church more often than its minister. He and Mozelle held the church together. Or did they just think they did?

As the group gathered, most of us visited the coffeepot in the corner of the room, and I passed the box of chocolates around. It held a variety of bonbons and truffles I'd collected from the discard tray at the chocolate shop. This didn't mean they weren't good—everything TenHuis Chocolade makes is delicious. No, it meant the Lemon Canache ("Tangy lemon interior with a dark chocolate coating") had been decorated with a flower, instead of two dark chocolate stripes and one yellow dot. Or that the Baileys Irish Cream bonbon ("Dark chocolate with a classic cream liqueur interior") was trimmed with milk chocolate, instead of a white chocolate. So we couldn't sell them, but all the creamy interiors and coatings would be delicious.

I had not brought any of the special WinterFest items my aunt Nettie, the owner of TenHuis Chocolade, was planning. She had to special order the molds with the WinterFest snowman logo, and they weren't due in for another twenty-four hours. I assured everyone that the snowmen would debut at the arts show opening Wednesday night.

Johnny Owens, who represented the Warner Pier Artists Association, came into the meeting next. He wore jeans and a flannel shirt, and his hair was in a buzz cut. Johnny was a sculptor who worked with a welding torch and sheet metal, but he also drew. His humorous doodles—cartoons and caricatures—were worthy of being framed. He had designed our snowman logo.

Johnny was followed by my favorite committee member, the mayor's representative, Joe Woodyard. Joe is a part-time city attorney, a part-time craftsman specializing in restoring antique motorboats, and a full-time husband—to me. He sat down beside me, and I was happy to get a pat on the shoulder and some eye contact from him. We hadn't parted on the best of terms that morning, but I wasn't mad any longer, and I hoped he wasn't either. I reached under the table and stroked his knee. Joe's a few inches taller than I am and has dark hair and blue eyes. I think he's the best-looking man in West

Michigan, but I'm prejudiced. Around Warner Pier he's still known as the guy who was state high school debate champ and state wrestling champ the same year.

Jason Foster, who was coordinating the food subcommittee, arrived, switching his long George Washington–style queue back and forth. He was followed by Sarajane Harding, who was in charge of the lodging for the promotion. Sarajane flashed her dimples at everyone. Sarajane is fiftyish. She always dressed in an almost masculine style, but had a very feminine face.

That was everybody on the committee except our chair, Ramona VanWinkle-Snow.

It was ten minutes past time for the meeting to begin, so I wasn't too surprised when Mozelle gave her papers a final twitch, cleared her throat, and spoke. "Perhaps we'd better not wait for Ramona." The virtuous tone of her voice was unmistakable.

Before I could say, "Let's give her another five minutes," the door opened, and Ramona came in like the blast of fresh air she had been to Warner Pier. She greeted us with "Welcome, fellow Michiganders!"

We replied according to our individual opinions on that label. George called out, "Michiganians!" Johnny Owens honked loudly, like a goose looking for a pond to light on. Maggie growled deep in her throat and said, "Personally, I'm a wolverine." I said, "Yeehaw! You can take the gal out of Texas, but you can't take Texas out of the gal." Mary Samson, Amos Hart, and Joe all grinned, and Mozelle gave a condescending smile that said, "Let the children have their fun." Ramona went to the last seat open, apologizing for being late.

"But I promise to have us out of here by five o'clock," she said.

Ramona looks like a leftover hippie. She wears her long

gray hair in a braid down the center of her back and dresses "artsy," in long print skirts, boots or sandals, and floppy sweaters.

Ramona's greeting was typical of the style she used to preside over our committee. The citizens of Michigan have never agreed on what to call themselves. Some prefer "Michigander" and some "Michiganian." Either is acceptable, I'm told, but we must never, ever use "Michiganite."

So at every meeting Ramona greeted us with one word or the other, preceding it with "fellow." The joke was that Ramona had been a "fellow" Michigander/Michiganian for only three years. She and her husband had bought a photography business and moved to Warner Pier from California about the time I came up from Texas. Ramona took care of the portrait side and was the business manager. Bob, her husband, was a more artistic photographer; I loved his dramatic landscapes, though I didn't love the prices they brought. He was frequently "best of show" in some exhibition.

Growing up in the Southwest, I'd always been told that Northerners—we called them "Yankees," even if they were not from New England—were not friendly. When I announced plans to move to my mother's hometown, my dad the Texan and his family advised against it. "You'll have to live there twenty years before anybody will even ignore you," my stepmother had said.

But I'd worked in Warner Pier as a teenager, and I still had friends I'd made then. My mother's family had lived in Warner Pier for seventy-five years. Plus, my aunt and employer, Nettie TenHuis, was a much-loved and respected citizen. By huddling under her wings, I had slid into the community like a hot knife through butter, making friends easily. A romance with Joe Woodyard hadn't hurt things; he'd grown up in Warner Pier and seemed to know all of the 2,500 people who lived there.

Ramona had not had those advantages, but she'd managed to become accepted in our small—sometimes too small—town even more easily than I had.

Ramona was intelligent, efficient, and tactful. She got things done. And if she was ignorant of the local situation, she turned that ignorance into an advantage.

Ramona called for a treasurer's report. I handed copies around the table, pointing out a few details I thought were important.

As usual, Ramona went straight to the point. "Then the only committee that's overbudget is the play," she said.

"That's because of the cost of the high school auditorium," Maggie said. "The school board isn't about to change its policy of refusing to forgive rent for nonschool functions, and I haven't been able to find an angel. I'm still trying to get a grant from the Adkins Foundation."

Mozelle made a noise just slightly too ladylike to be a snort. "The Adkins Foundation will only assist school-related projects," she said. "You're wasting your time there."

"I may have been able to help," Ramona said. "Charles Adkins was in our shop last week, so I approached him about it."

"Oh!" Mozelle's voice was scandalized. "Oh, Ramona! We don't want to anger the Adkins Foundation. That could do the community untold harm!"

Ramona looked at her blandly. "I don't think it hurt anything, Mozelle. I described our plans to him, emphasizing the educational aspect and the student participation. And he wrote a note for me to send along with a new application. He's only one board member, of course, but if we have his backing—well, I'm hopeful."

Mozelle had trouble keeping her virtuous smile. Ramona had turned her newcomer status into an advantage. In the past, Mozelle, aware of the Adkins Foundation's strict policy, had been afraid to approach that body. Ramona had made it seem as if she were blundering in out of ignorance, and it looked as if she was going to score some money.

Ramona was too tactful to gloat. She turned to the next report. "George, how's the art show shaping up?"

"Just fine," George said. "Most of the entries are here already, and I've arranged to hang the show on Tuesday." He looked at Jason Foster. The art show was to be held at the conference center.

Jason nodded. "Tuesday should be fine. Talk to me after the meeting if you need ladders and such. The partitions are set up and ready to arrange."

"Right." George turned back to Ramona. "There's a small crisis over the juror, but that seems to be settled." He explained the change in jurors to the rest of the committee.

"If you're satisfied with the new man's credentials, that's fine," Ramona said. "Who is he?"

George began to look through his papers. "He taught art at several colleges in the Washington, D.C., area, but he's now retired. His own work is mainly in acrylics. He's an experienced juror." He pulled a paper out of the pile.

"Here's his résumé, if anybody wants to see it. His name is Fletcher Mendenhall."

I'd never heard of him, so I didn't react. And no one else did either for about five seconds.

Then Johnny Owens laughed.

Chapter 2

I happened to be looking at Mozelle when Johnny laughed, and she closed her eyes, looking even more like insulted virtue than usual. Her let's-be-serious attitude was hard to take.

George's reaction was different. He looked concerned. "Do you know Fletcher Mendenhall?"

Johnny got to his feet and walked over to the coffeepot. "I was at Waterford College when Fletcher Mendenhall was teaching there."

"Is there something we should know about him?"

"He's a shrimpy little guy with a big mouth. But he was a good teacher, and he ought to be fine as a juror."

"Why did you laugh when you heard his name?"

Johnny concentrated on picking up a coffee cup. "I shouldn't have laughed. Hearing his name reminded me of a funny incident."

Ramona looked at Johnny steadily. "Can you share it?"

"It was stupid. Just a prank. Undergraduate humor at its worst. Origin of the word 'sophomoric.' "

Ramona didn't speak. She just kept waiting. Johnny cleared his throat. He poured coffee, he sipped it, and he finally spoke.

"There was this trustee, see—a trustee of the college. He

was pushing for big budget cuts, and he'd singled out the art department. We were all mad at him. There was a demonstration. College-kid stuff."

"How did Fletcher Mendenhall fit in?"

"A faculty art show was held about then, and Dr. Mendenhall exhibited a nude. Representational. An acrylic. The model was posed so that her face wasn't visible. Well—this nude was shapely, and she had a birthmark on her fanny. And the word got around fast that the trustee's wife had a birthmark like that one. All the students thought it was funny."

Ramona frowned. "The implication being that Mendenhall must have seen the trustee's wife's fanny."

"Yeah. Of course, if she did have a birthmark, Mendenhall could have learned about it from someone who saw her at the gym or something."

"But it wasn't very tactful," Ramona said. "What happened to Mendenhall?"

"Nothing. The trustee couldn't gripe about the birthmark without admitting his wife had one like it."

"And that would have been more humiliating than the painting."

"Right." Johnny looked at his cup. "I said it was undergraduate humor."

"I can see why college kids would think it was funny, but it seems a bit immature for a professor," I said. "And the joke was a little hard on Mrs. Trustee."

"I guess we didn't think about her. She was a second, very young, wife the trustee had recently acquired. A former Waterford student. A trophy wife."

I felt as if Johnny had slapped me, but I guess I was able to hide my reaction until I spoke.

"I guess we're not hiring a juror to be a dipsomaniac," I said. "I mean, a diplomat!"

Rats! I only get my words twisted when I'm nervous. Would Johnny guess that he'd upset me?

Amos Hart was the only person who tittered openly at my slip of the tongue. All these people knew me so well that they overlooked my habit of getting my tongue tangled, though Mozelle did give the first genuine-looking smile she'd smiled yet.

I tried to go on as if I hadn't made a fool of myself. "Does an art show juror have any public chores to do?"

"No," George said. "He has to come here to Warner Pier, look at the show firsthand, and name the winners."

"Dr. Mendenhall can do that," Johnny said. "He's a very sound artist. And he was a good teacher."

"He's flying in Tuesday," George said. "If we change jurors again, we'd have to find somebody from around here."

"And that's not a good idea," Ramona said briskly. "Mendenhall's jokes of years ago are no reason to reject him." She turned to the next committee member. "Amos, how is the chorale coming along?"

I listened with half an ear, hoping that nobody had caught on to how much the mention of a "trophy wife" had upset me. I told myself that Johnny wouldn't have used the term if he'd known I was sensitive on the subject.

I didn't know Johnny very well. He had no way of knowing I'd spent five years as a trophy wife. Everybody in Warner Pier knew that both Joe and I had been married before. And our friends all knew that both of us had been married to people older than we were. That was stale gossip. There was no reason Johnny Owens would know more than that.

I came back to the meeting mentally when Mary Samson handed me invoices for advertising she'd authorized. I reminded everyone they should turn in any other invoices as soon as possible, and Ramona asked if we were ready to adjourn.

"One more thing," George said. "I'm hanging the art show on Tuesday, and Mendenhall is flying into Grand Rapids at four that afternoon. I can't be two places at once, so we need someone to pick him up. Any volunteers?"

We all whipped out pocket calendars, and Joe was the first person to speak. "I have to be in Grand Rapids for an update on city finance laws that day. I ought to be through in time to pick him up."

"Joe would be the perfect escort for Dr. Mendenhall," Johnny said, grinning again.

I didn't understand his comment, but I didn't ask for an explanation. George promised to e-mail Mendenhall's flight information and cell phone number to Joe, and the meeting ended—at four fifty-five p.m. Ramona had gotten us out before five o'clock. Or she would have if Mozelle hadn't decided to drop a minor bombshell.

Joe was giving me a ride, so Maggie left without me. Ramona, Mozelle, Joe, and I were the only people still there when Mozelle spoke.

"Ramona, I can't do any more of the television and radio interviews."

I stared at Mozelle in complete astonishment. We'd all applauded Ramona's tact in giving her the job as WinterFest spokesman. It was the perfect job for a past chair who was on the committee only as a courtesy. She was allowed to appear publicly, but she didn't have to do any real work.

Mozelle had done interviews with all the Grand Rapids and Kalamazoo television stations, and she'd even been quoted in the *Chicago Tribune* and the *Detroit Free Press*. She had pretended to resent the inconvenience, but it had obviously fed her ego. And now she was quitting?

Joe looked as amazed as I felt, and Ramona gave a little gasp. "Oh, Mozelle!" she said. "You've done such a good job. And you're nearly through. Don't stop now."

"I'm afraid I must," Mozelle said.

Ramona looked distressed. "Have we offended you in some way?"

"No! No! Not at all. The WinterFest is a wonderful project. I'm not withdrawing my support from it."

"But you are, Mozelle. Unless you're in the hospital—and I mean for something serious—it's going to look awfully funny if you stop working on the project now. Why are you doing this?"

"I'm sorry, Ramona. I truly am. But it's a personal matter. I'm going to have to go on a trip, a business trip."

"A business trip?"

I felt as incredulous as Ramona sounded. Mozelle didn't work. When a group of Warner Pier women formed an investment club, she had declined to join on the grounds that all her capital was in bonds, which she left in the hands of a Holland investment firm. What business did she have that would take her out of town?

"It's family business," she said. "I'm terribly sorry, but I'll have to be gone this weekend." Nodding regally, she went out the door with the aplomb of Queen Elizabeth II entering Westminster Abbey.

Ramona shook her head as she headed for the door. "Just when you think you've heard everything, you find out you haven't. I'll see you two later."

Joe and I were close behind her. "Before I go home, I'd better go by the office to check my e-mail," I said.

"I can handle dinner."

"I wouldn't say no."

I knew Joe's menu would be frozen lasagna, but that was okay with me as long as I didn't have to cook it.

Joe and I didn't have much to say before he dropped me at TenHuis Chocolade, where my minivan was parked. We had both said too much over breakfast that morning. I was hoping that his offer to cook dinner was a sign that he felt bad about the remarks that had flown around over the oatmeal. I knew I felt bad about my share of them.

Mozelle's sudden resignation from the WinterFest committee—a committee no one had wanted her to serve on in the first place—mystified me only slightly as I drove home forty-five minutes later. I was more concerned with Joe and our relationship. We'd each had one bad marriage. We both wanted a good one this time around.

Our current problem was financial. Oh, we had enough money to get by on. We just weren't agreed on how to spend it. And our first Christmas together was coming, and with it the challenge of buying presents.

I've never denied that I'm warped about money. My parents were always in debt, and as a child I lay in bed night after night and listened to arguments echoing down the hall. And nearly all those arguments were over how to pay the bills. When my parents divorced the year I was sixteen, I blamed financial problems for their split. Recently I'd discovered there was a lot more to the story, but it was too late. I'll always be warped about money.

I can't stand to owe anybody a cent. I can't bear it, endure it, tolerate it, or put up with it. I'm not quite sane on the matter.

Joe's attitude about debt is more matter-of-fact, maybe more normal. He sees debt as something to manage, not completely avoid.

When my aunt, Nettie TenHuis, married Warner Pier's police chief, Hogan Jones, the previous June, she gave Joe and me the TenHuis family home, a hundred-year-old frame house on the inland side of Lake Shore Drive. The prospect of owning a house with no mortgage attached thrilled me.

Joe, however, immediately decided we should build on a

second bathroom and expand the kitchen to hold a dish-washer. I'd gone along with it—he was the guy with the power tools—but I'd specified that we were to get a bank loan, not use credit cards. So before the first Visa payment came due, I had arranged the home-improvement loan, and we were able to pay for our home expansion on what I considered a busi-nesslike schedule.

Now, six months later, I had discovered that Joe had put tile, lumber, and other items on the Visa card he used for busi-ness expenses. That card was loaded, and it was not all stuff for Joe's boat shop.

Never open your mail before breakfast. I'd opened his Visa bill—I'd mistaken it for the household bill—at seven thirty, When I began to howl about it, the whole discussion morphed into an argument about why Joe had hidden that bill from me and how much to spend on Christmas and a lot of other points, all of them sore.

The whole thing had gotten my day off to a really bad start. I hoped the day's ending would be better.

I smelled smoke as I got out of the van in our drive, and through the living room window I could see Joe kneeling in front of the fireplace. I smiled. We didn't usually take time for a fire on a weeknight, but Joe knew I loved having one any-time. So building a fire was a calming gesture.

When Joe greeted me at the door with a glass of wine, I knew he was in major peacemaking mode. I accepted the wine, and the kiss that went with it.

Then I looked at the glass. "Hmmm. White? You usually open a bottle of red to go with lasagna."

"We're not having lasagna. I went by the Dock Street Pizza Place and picked up two orders of chicken marsala."

I must have blinked. Our budget limits our dinners out. But before I could swallow my comment, Joe kissed me again. "And I didn't put it on a credit card," he said.

So the evening turned out pretty well. We were able to discuss our misunderstanding over the credit cards and we both admitted we'd been wrong—Joe for putting stuff for the house on his business card and me for shouting about it. We discussed Christmas fairly rationally, though Joe refused to commit to my proposal to limit our gifts for each other to the living room couch we'd already ordered. We agreed that we'd renegotiate the home-improvement loan with my pal Barbara to pay off the house items that had shown up on the business card, though Joe asked me to wait until after Christmas. After we'd eaten, we enjoyed using the new dishwasher. It was the next morning before the WinterFest interrupted our lives again.

Joe looked at his pocket calendar at the breakfast table. "I'm afraid I volunteered to pick up that art show juror on Tuesday," he said.

"I'm afraid you did."

"Can I borrow your van?"

I laughed. "Yes, though a vehicle I use for hauling chocolate isn't much of an improvement on one you use for hauling boats."

Joe's transportation is a pickup truck with the name of his boat restoration business, Vintage Boats, painted on the side. His old truck had died two months earlier, and the new one burned diesel fuel and had a manual transmission, because that was the truck he got the best deal on.

"I hate to leave you 'in the clutch,' " he said. "I know you're not used to the manual transmission."

"My daddy the mechanic taught me to drive a stick shift, and I haven't forgotten how. I won't be driving very far or in heavy traffic."

Several days went by. People dropped invoices for WinterFest expenses by the office, but I had nothing to do with the final preparations for the event, and at the shop we were busy shipping out last-minute Christmas orders and getting ready for the next big chocolate holiday, Valentine's Day, two months away.

The biggest event was the arrival of the molds for the snowman logo for WinterFest. Aunt Nettie ran some samples, and they looked good. There were dark, milk, and white pastilles—those are rectangles of flat, molded chocolate—with tiny snowmen in relief. They were shown playing musical instruments and painting pictures and singing. There were also three-dimensional snowmen in four-inch and eight-inch sizes. Again, these carried artistic props such as paintbrushes, palettes, musical instruments, and masks representing comedy and drama. They wore multicolored scarves, which had to be hand-painted of tinted white chocolate. Everyone at the shop thought they were delightful. We were careful to keep them hidden from the public, since Aunt Nettie planned to unveil them at the art show opening on Wednesday. We did give Johnny Owens a peek, since the logo he'd designed had inspired them.

Aunt Nettie was also making a giant snowman that would be used as a centerpiece for the refreshment table at the art show opening, the first WinterFest event.

Tuesday morning arrived before I was ready, and when Joe came out wearing his pin-striped lawyer suit, instead of the work clothes he wears to the boat shop, I had trouble remembering why. Then I handed him the keys to the van, accepted the keys to the truck, and kissed him good-bye as he left for Grand Rapids.

At a few minutes after three that afternoon I was concentrating on accounts receivable when the phone rang, and I saw Joe's cell phone number on the caller ID.

He sounded urgent. "Lee, I've got an emergency here."

"What's wrong?"

"The attorney general's coming to our meeting. He

wants to talk to us about the proposed city finance bill. But he's not here yet. I can't leave before he comes, and I'm supposed to be at the airport to pick up that Dr. Mendenhall in an hour."

"I'll go get him."

"Surely there's someone else on the committee. George . . ."

"George is busy hanging that show. I'll go."

"You don't like to drive that truck. . . ."

"I'll borrow Aunt Nettie's car. Hogan won't mind picking her up."

We left it at that. But the minute I hung up, I remembered that Aunt Nettie was in Holland for a doctor's appointment. I couldn't borrow her car.

Mendenhall's plane was due at four, and I was an hour from the airport. I needed to leave ten minutes ago.

I opened Joe's e-mail, found the message George had sent telling him Mendenhall's time of arrival and cell phone number, and printed it out. I called to Dolly Jolly, Aunt Nettie's chief assistant, to explain why I was leaving. I grabbed up a box of the WinterFest snowmen to present to Dr. Mendenhall as I welcomed him. I put on my ski jacket over my jeans and turtleneck and was out the door at three twenty.

Luckily, I didn't run into unusual traffic, and the roads were clear of snow. But I knew I was not going to be at the airport in time to park the truck and go inside to greet Mendenhall graciously as he came down the corridor from the gate. I'd have to call him.

As soon as I felt sure Mendenhall's plane was on the ground, I grabbed out my cell phone, hoping I wasn't in one of the numerous dead spots that dot the shore of Lake Michigan—such as the Warner Point Conference Center, where cell phones won't work at all.

I punched in Mendenhall's cell number, eager to assure him that he hadn't been abandoned.

When Mendenhall answered, his hello didn't sound too upset.

"Dr. Mendenhall? This is Lee Woodyard, from the Warner Pier WinterFest committee. I'm on my way to pick you up, but I'm running a bit late."

"That's quite all right, young lady. Did you say your name is Lee?"

"Yes. I'm about twenty minutes from the airport."

"Twenty minutes is exactly the time I need to recover from the flight, Lee."

"That's wonderful! Shall I just pull up outside?"

"I'll get my luggage and meet you at the pickup area closest to American Airlines. How will I know you?"

"I'll be in a blue GMC truck. My husband was to pick you up, but he had an emersion—I mean, an emergency! He got stuck elsewhere, so I'm the filter. I mean, fill-in!"

Mendenhall laughed, which is the usual way people react to my twisted tongue. "I'll be waiting," he said.

He wasn't mad. I breathed a sigh of relief, but I didn't slow down. As I entered Gerald Ford International Airport, I almost skidded to a stop at the security booth, and I whipped out my cell phone to call Mendenhall again while the guard was looking at my driver's license.

"Helloo!" Dr. Mendenhall's voice sounded even more cheerful than it had twenty minutes earlier.

"This is Lee Woodyard again. I'll be at the American pickup area in about thirty seconds."

"Land ho, Lee! I won't be there when you pull up, but I'll be there almost immediately."

"They won't let me wait too long, Dr. Mendenhall."

"I know, I know. Airport security men are not rule breakers. What did you say you look like?"

"I'll be in a blue GMC pickup."

"You, my dear. Not your vehicle."

"I'm wearing a red ski jacket and jeans, Dr. Mendenhall. I don't have a hat on. I'm tall, and I have blond hair."

He chuckled. "You sound enticing. I'll hurry."

The phone went dead, the security man handed my driver's license back, and I slowly drove forward toward the pickup area at the curb. I parked in the correct spot, realizing that I'd failed to ask Mendenhall what he looked like. I remembered that Johnny Owens had described him as "shrimpy," so I scanned the area for a small guy.

But the man who came through the automatic doors nearest me wasn't exactly small. He was short, true, but he was round. He had on a padded khaki jacket that made him look even shorter and rounder than he really was. A blue-and-brown wool scarf was draped around his neck, and a light blue stocking cap covered his head. He was dragging a small wheeled suitcase.

Mendenhall looked amazingly like the logo for the Win-terFest, right down to the merry grin.

I got out of the pickup and went to meet him. I held out my hand in shaking position, realizing that I towered over the man by at least six inches. "Dr. Mendenhall?"

"Call me Fletch, young lady. And you must be Lee."

"I'm terribly sorry to be late picking you up."

Mendenhall gave that fruity chuckle I'd heard on the phone. "No matter. I had business to transact before I could leave the airport. Your timing is perfect."

I opened the passenger's door and took Mendenhall's suitcase from him. It was small enough to slip behind the passenger's seat, so I shoved it in there. Mendenhall climbed into the cab of the truck, and I went around to the driver's side. I buckled up and pulled away as quickly as possible, mindful of airport rules about lingering too long at the curb.

I was on the exit road before I turned to Mendenhall again. He took his knitted hat off and gave me a goofy grin.

Then he put out a hand, holding a flat metal container toward me.

"Can I offer you a little drink?" he said. His eyes were slightly unfocused.

The man was as drunk as a skunk.

Chapter 3

Dr. Fletcher Mendenhall, I realized, had used the twenty minutes he had to wait for me to visit the airport bar. In fact, as I looked at his bleary eyes, I became convinced that he hadn't visited only the airport bar. He'd had a good head start before his plane landed.

He was leaning ever closer to me—barely restrained by his seat belt—and was still offering me the old-fashioned flat metal flask.

"Just a little drink?" he said.

"No, thank you," I said. "I don't drink while I'm driving."

"Oh." He sounded terribly hurt. "A little one won't hurt you."

"I need to concentrate on driving my husband's truck," I said.

Dr. Mendenhall leaned back in his corner and sighed. Maybe he was going to be a docile drunk. Maybe he wouldn't be a problem while I drove him to Warner Pier, an hour away down a wintry Michigan highway. Maybe.

How should I handle this? Was silence the best method? Or should I use casual talk to give the drive a semblance of normalcy?

I never really decided which was the best method. I simply couldn't sit there without talking. So I began to tell Mendenhall why my husband hadn't picked him up. I managed the story pretty well, except that I said Joe was in a meeting with the "atonal generator" instead of the "attorney general." And maybe I emphasized the word "husband" more than necessary. I wanted to make sure Mendenhall knew I had one.

My talk made no difference to Mendenhall. He leaned back in his corner and didn't seem to be paying attention. I began to relax. After all, as Johnny Owens had said, Mendenhall was just a little shrimp. I was six inches taller than he was, even if he was a lot bigger around. And he was acting quite meek. I tried to convince myself that I could deliver him to Sarajane Foster's B and B with no trouble to either of us. Then he'd be *her* problem. Or could I do that to Sarajane?

That plan might have worked, if it hadn't been rush hour. Just after we merged onto Interstate 196, which leads south to Warner Pier, traffic came to a complete stop.

The lack of movement seemed to rouse Mendenhall. He sat up. "Where are we?"

"South of Grand Rapids. Traffic is heavy this afternoon."

He offered me the flask again. "Now that we're stopped, you can take your hands off the wheel and have a drink."

"No, thanks."

He unbuckled his seat belt. "At least I can get comfortable."

"Please keep your seat belt on, Dr. Mendenhall. Michigan is very strict about that. I don't want to get pulled over."

"A pretty girl like you could talk your way out of a ticket."

"I wouldn't want to try. And if I have to stop in a hurry, I might toss you through the windshield." I didn't add that that prospect sounded quite enticing.

Mendenhall slid toward me. "You're too pretty to be so standoffish. Have a drink."

"No."

At that moment traffic began to move again, and I concentrated on the clutch and the gearshift of the unfamiliar truck. I ignored Mendenhall. Maybe he'd get the idea.

Once traffic began to move, it accelerated fast. For a mile I was fully occupied in driving. Then my lane slowed suddenly, and I had to downshift.

That was when I realized that Mendenhall had moved toward me, sliding across the seat. I was too worried about a semi on my left to look at him, but I spoke firmly. "Dr. Mendenhall, please buckle your seat belt."

"Oh, come on, young lady. I can't be friendly clear over on the other side of this truck."

I was downshifting from third to second—with both hands and both feet extremely busy—when he ran his hand along the inside of my knee.

My reflexes took over. I put all my strength behind a vigorous jab with my right elbow that caught him in the shoulder. "Get back in your seat belt!"

Mendenhall moved away, though not as far away as I would have liked.

I sneaked a glance at him. He was rubbing his shoulder and looking wounded. If he wanted sympathy, he was out of luck. I was wishing my elbow had had a spear point attached.

Traffic slowed almost to a stop again. We were barely moving, and I tried to watch Mendenhall out of the corner of my eye.

He was still rubbing his shoulder. "That wasn't very friendly. When I visit a new place, I like to be friendly."

"Pawing at a woman who is not eager for your attentions is not friendly. Please buckle your seat belt and stay on your side of the cab, Dr. Mendenhall."

He took another nip from his flask, pouting. He did not

put his seat belt on. Traffic inched along. I was imprisoned in the truck. I began to make plans for breaking out of that prison.

We passed a sign saying it would be a mile before the next exit, one long mile before I could get off the interstate.

I allowed myself to hope that Mendenhall would subside. Pass out. Catch on to the idea I was trying to put across.

Unfortunately, the idea he got was not the one I had in mind. Traffic began to move a little faster, but we'd barely gone a hundred feet—I was shifting from first to second—when Mendenhall slid across the seat and leaned toward me.

"Now, Lee, I know you can be friendly. A beautiful woman like you knows she's attractive to men. You must enjoy the attention."

He got up on his knees in the seat, leaned over, and breathed down my neck.

"Get away!" As soon as I could get my hand off the gearshift, I put my palm in the enter of his chest and pushed him over backward. "Stay away from me!"

He chuckled. "You know you like it."

Just then I saw the promise of deliverance. It was one of those highway signs describing which services are available at exits.

There was a motel at the next exit, I saw, and that exit was now close. I slid the truck into the exit lane without bothering to make a turn signal.

Mendenhall was getting up onto his knees, apparently ready for another try at my nape, and my sudden swerve almost threw him into the dashboard. As soon as he regained his balance, he began to crawl across the seat toward me. I again put my palm in the center of his chest. This time I pushed gently.

"If you're feeling this amorous," I said, "you need to get a room."

The guy nearly fell over backward, and it wasn't because of my push. He was flatly astonished. "A room?"

"Yes. There's a motel at this exit. They rent rooms. Do you have a credit card?"

"A credit card?"

"To pay for the room."

"The room?"

He sounded scared to death. Dr. Fletcher Mendenhall was confirming something I'd long suspected. These creeps who come on so hard with no encouragement don't really want to succeed. They're simply trying to embarrass the object of the chase. Something about me—could it be my height?—had intimidated Mendenhall. He had no sexual interest in me at all. He simply felt that he had to humiliate me.

I wasn't humiliated. I was furious. And we were about to find out who wound up embarrassed.

We reached the bottom of the exit ramp, and an arrow on another highway department sign showed me which way to turn. I made a hard right, drove a block, and turned into the driveway of a budget motel chain. It looked sleazy enough for my purpose.

The truck skidded slightly as I hit the brakes in front of the office. I turned to face Mendenhall and smiled. "Okay. Get a room."

A broad smile came over the professor's face. Once again he offered me his old-fashioned flask. This time I took it from him, though I didn't drink from it. The idea of touching my lips to something that Mendenhall's mouth had been on was nauseating. I could barely stand to hold it in my hand.

"I'll keep this," I said. "You go in and get a room."

Instead, he leaned toward me, apparently deciding my new attitude deserved a kiss.

Again, I gently shoved him away with my palm. "Get a room."

He almost fell getting out of the truck, and he staggered slightly as he went into the office. As soon as he was inside, I grabbed my phone and tried to call Joe. His phone was out of service. I debated throwing Mendenhall's suitcase out right there, but by the time I'd left a message for Joe, Mendenhall was coming back out. I put the phone away.

Mendenhall got into the truck and held up a key card. "Around to the right," he said, "and I want to assure you that I consider myself a very lucky man."

"What's the room number?"

"One twenty-two."

"Good. You're on the ground floor."

There was a parking spot in front of 122, and I pulled into it. Mendenhall got out and went to the door. By the time he'd fumbled through opening it—he tried at least four times before he got the card in the slot the right way up—I had taken his suitcase out from behind the seat.

He turned around, smiling, and motioned for me to precede him into the room.

I crossed the walkway and dropped the suitcase in front of him. I handed him the flask. I presented him with the box of chocolate snowmen I'd forgotten to give him earlier.

"Good-bye," I said.

Then I got back in the truck and locked the doors. Mendenhall was still standing there, looking stupid, as I backed out of my parking place.

I rolled the window down a few inches and yelled through it. "Someone will pick you up in the morning!" Then I drove off.

I was halfway back to the office before Mendenhall ran after me, shaking his fist. I could see his lips move, but I was too far away to understand what he was saying.

Leaving the motel, I turned right so that I wouldn't have to wait for traffic to clear. This meant I had to turn around in the parking lot of the supermarket across the street to head back to I-196, but I did not want to linger on the motel grounds.

Once I was on I-196, headed toward Warner Pier, the pace of traffic had picked up, and I was able to drive at top speed for five miles. My phone rang twice, but when I checked the number, I saw it was the one I'd called to reach Mendenhall. I turned the phone off.

I pulled off at an exit that advertised a McDonald's. I went inside, ordered a cup of coffee, sat down at a table, and shook. I don't know if the shaking was caused by nervousness or fury.

After a couple of sips of caffeine, I turned my phone back on and tried to call Joe again. Still no answer. Mendenhall hadn't left a message, and he had apparently quit trying to reach me. I scanned the numbers I had saved in my cell phone. I didn't have George Jenkins' number, and I needed to tell him I'd dumped his juror. I found Ramona's number, however, and she needed to be told, too. I called her, but she wasn't answering. I didn't leave a message. Somehow I didn't want a permanent record of anything I might say at that moment.

By then I'd stopped shaking, and I remembered that Joe kept a Warner County phone book in his truck. I put the lid on my coffee, got back in the vehicle, found the phone book, and called George Jenkins. He didn't answer either.

Sarajane Foster needed to know she'd have an empty room at the B and B that night, and I tried to call her. No answer there, either, but the answering machine picked up. I left a message saying Mendenhall wouldn't be there until the next day, but I didn't explain why. I simply said he was staying in Grand Rapids that night.

Since it was then after five p.m., in December, in Michigan, the sun was down. I drove on home. The drive was not improved when it began to snow enough to slow traffic.

I don't like driving in snow, but I wasn't sorry to have something to worry about besides my run-in with Dr. Fletcher Mendenhall and my frustrated attempts to tell somebody what had happened.

Mad as I was, I was sensible enough to know that I didn't want to tell the whole world. I had to assume that Mendenhall would sober up and fulfill his responsibilities as judge of the WinterFest art show. There was no purpose in humiliating George Jenkins and the WinterFest committee by making the out-of-town jerk's transgressions generally known.

So, when the phone rang as soon as I got in the house, I let the answering machine catch it. I snatched the receiver up as soon as I heard Joe's voice.

"Pal, you are in trouble," I said. "I'm not doing any more airport pickups for you."

"What happened?"

I gave him the full story, with embellishments. Joe's only comments were along the line of "You're kidding" and "I can't believe this," with one angry "I'll kill the guy."

However, when I got to the description of Mendenhall running along the motel sidewalk, shaking his fist as I drove off, Joe blew it. He laughed.

"This is not funny!"

"I know, Lee. I'm just so darn proud of you."

"You'd better be!"

"I am. That was quick thinking. Mendenhall deserved to be dumped in the snow out on the interstate. He deserved to be run over by a semi and flattened as flat as—as one of his acrylics. You handled it great."

I felt somewhat mollified. "What do we do now?"

"I guess I'd better check on him. I'm still in Grand Rapids, so I'll stop on my way out of town."

I told Joe the exit, the motel, and the room number. "I think you ought to leave him there tonight," I said. "I left a message telling Sarajane he wouldn't be at her B and B to-night. I can't imagine that Mendenhall could have sobered up enough that she'd be willing to have him as a guest. She's in the place alone this time of the year. George may have to find him another place to stay."

Joe promised to call after he'd stopped to check on Mendenhall. I began to think about dinner, although the snow might make him late getting home.

About twenty minutes later, Joe called again. He started by repeating the exit number, motel name, and room number.

"Room one twenty-two," I said. "I'm sure that's right. Isn't he there?"

"I think he may have passed out. I banged on the door, but he didn't answer. So I called his cell phone, and I can hear it ring—or peal; he's got the 'Hallelujah Chorus' on it. But he's not answering."

"Could he have gone out for dinner? There's a restaurant next door."

"He doesn't sound as if he would be thinking about food, but I'll check everything within walking distance. I guess I'd better quiz the desk clerk, too. I'll make sure Mendenhall didn't call a cab."

But when Joe got home an hour and a half later, he said Mendenhall hadn't been at any nearby restaurant, and the desk clerk claimed that he knew nothing about him. Apparently no cab had come to the motel.

"Let's forget him," he said. "He probably passed out. I'll go back first thing tomorrow morning."

I called Ramona and George all evening, as late as ten o'clock, but neither of them ever answered at their homes, and Ramona's cell phone was turned off. I didn't have George's cell number.

I was surprised by this lack of interest in where our juror was and why he hadn't been delivered to Warner Pier. But I didn't worry about it. Mendenhall was safely stowed away—unless he decided to leave his motel—and my responsibility was over. Joe could take it from here.

And he did. At eight fifteen the next morning, I heard him asking the motel clerk to connect him with room 122. But he didn't say anything else.

When I brought the coffee to the breakfast table, I said, "Is Mendenhall too hungover to answer the phone?"

"I guess so. I've tried his cell phone and the motel phone, but he's not answering either."

"I hope he didn't take a cab back to the airport and go home, or that he's not sick. Dead would be okay."

Joe laughed. "I'll go up there as soon as I finish breakfast. You get hold of George. I'm sure he expected Mendenhall to judge the show today."

"If he's as hungover as he deserves to be, I pity the artists."

We left it at that. And that morning I was able to catch George Jenkins, who was properly shocked and apologetic about my experience. He was also relieved to hear that Joe had gone back to Grand Rapids to bring Mendenhall down.

He apologized for not being available by phone the evening before. "I had to run into Holland," he said.

I went on to the office. An hour later I was immersed in an order for fifty large Valentine hearts filled with tiny cupids, a special design for a Detroit gift shop, when the phone rang. I saw Joe's number on the caller ID.

"Howdy," I said. "Is Mendenhall on his feet?"

Joe didn't answer for a long moment. "Not really."

"Don't tell me he's still drunk!"

"No. He's not drunk. But you'd better clear your calendar for today. You probably should come up here to make a statement."

"A statement! That jerk had better not be filing some sort of complaint!"

"No, Mendenhall doesn't have any complaint."

"Then what's going on?"

"He didn't answer when I banged on his door, so I got the desk clerk to open up. Mendenhall's lying on the floor. He's dead."

"Oh, no! If he wasn't drunk yesterday—if he was sick and I abandoned him, I'll never forgive myself."

"Sick or drunk, it doesn't really matter. His prior condition doesn't seem to have anything to do with his death."

"What happened to him?"

"Somebody bashed his head in with the desk lamp, Lee. It looks like murder."

Chapter 4

I was clear out onto Peach Street, headed for the interstate, before I thought of George Jenkins. I might not have thought of him then if I hadn't driven past his business, Peach Street Gallery of Art.

"Oh, my gosh!" I was so startled I spoke out loud. "George has lost another juror."

I wheeled the van into the curb and ran for the door. The gallery wasn't open yet, but I could see movement, so I pounded on the glass until George came to let me in, looking astonished. "Lee?"

"Did Joe call you? Just now?"

"No, Joe hasn't called today."

"Then you haven't heard about Mendenhall."

George rolled his eyes. "What now?"

I refused to come inside, so George and I stood on the sidewalk, and I told him that Joe had found the art show juror beaten to death. "I thought you needed to know right away," I said.

George grabbed his head with both hands. "I know I should be shocked and horrified, but all I can think about is how I'll find another juror."

"That," I said, "is your problem. Sorry to dump it on you

and run, George, but Joe says I need to come up there and make a statement."

"Yes, I see that." George shook his head. "I hope they figure out what happened. He did sound peculiar when he called last night."

"Did you talk to him?"

"No. He left a message on my cell."

I drove to Grand Rapids as quickly as possible, and I used the forty-five minutes it took to get there to worry.

Mendenhall was dead? Beaten to death with a desk lamp? I found it hard to believe.

If Joe had told me the death looked like a heart attack, or like an overdose, or like a stroke, I wouldn't have been surprised. I might have felt a bit guilty for leaving him alone in a motel in a strange city. But I definitely wasn't responsible if he'd been beaten to death with a desk lamp.

But however Mendenhall died, there was no reason I should feel responsible at all, I told myself. After all, Mendenhall was a grown man. If he had become ill, he had been alert enough to call an ambulance, or he had been when I left him. And if he chose to drink himself into a stupor, that wasn't my fault.

But he'd been beaten to death? How could it have happened? Who could have done such a thing?

I was in such a state of nerves that I asked myself that question for twenty minutes before I saw the answer that the police were going to jump on right away.

The cops were going to think I'd done it. Or else they were going to think Joe had done it.

Yikes!

I could well be the person to admit last seeing Mendenhall alive, and my husband had been at the motel looking for him later that evening.

Joe and I were very likely in big trouble. We were certain to be at the head of the suspect list.

I had dumped Mendenhall at the motel, then called my husband to complain that the man had offered me unwanted attentions, attentions obnoxious enough that I had refused to drive another forty-five minutes with him. I could easily be suspected of using physical force to repel those attentions.

Hard on the heels of learning that Mendenhall hadn't exactly treated me with respect, Joe had gone to Mendenhall's room looking for him. Someone who didn't know Joe could easily picture him in the classic role of angry husband.

There was no hiding either situation. The desk clerk had seen me in the truck as Mendenhall went in to rent a room. Later Joe had gone to the desk clerk to try to find Mendenhall. The clerk was almost certain to remember one or both of us. Joe had also checked out restaurants in the area, looking for Mendenhall. Somebody was going to remember that, too.

To add to the confusion, the crime had happened in a suburb of Grand Rapids, not in our friendly hometown of Warner Pier, where Joe and I were well-known residents. Heck, in Warner Pier the chief of police was my uncle by marriage. Hogan Jones looked on me almost as a daughter, and he and Joe were good friends. He knew us both well enough to feel sure we wouldn't beat anybody to death—no matter how obnoxious the guy had been.

But I had a feeling that being related to the chief of police in a town of 2,500 was not going to cut a lot of ice with the police in another, larger city.

Joe had been a defense attorney. He would know how to handle the situation.

So the first goal I had as I drove toward Grand Rapids was to talk to Joe. This didn't turn out to be a simple thing to do.

When I got to the motel, it was surrounded by police cars, all with lights flashing, and an ambulance was around at the side of the motel, near room 122. My first surprise was that the emergency vehicles had "Lake Knapp" painted on their doors. The motel where I'd dumped Mendenhall was in a city that I'd never even noticed on the map.

A uniformed patrolman was keeping cars from entering the drive. I finally parked in the lot of the shopping center across the street and walked to the motel through the slush, trying not to fall down in the gutter.

After I got to the motel, of course, no one had told the patrolmen guarding the drive to expect me. They wouldn't let me in, even when I said I was there to make a statement.

I called Joe's cell phone. It was turned off, but I left a message telling him I was freezing my tootsies outside the motel. I added that I'd go to the chain restaurant next door, drink something hot, and wait.

I'd barely been served a cup of coffee when a handsome blond guy wearing a bulky overcoat came in. He looked around the restaurant, brushed the hostess aside, and came to my booth. He had an air of complete confidence, an air some women find attractive. I am not one of those women. Not anymore. My ex-husband had that air.

The man displayed a giant mouthful of teeth and offered me a badge instead of a handshake. "I'm Detective Van Robertson," he said. "Are you Mrs. Woodyard?"

I nodded and prepared to get up, assuming he'd want me to go back to the motel. Instead Robertson sat down. Beside me. On my side of the booth. Boxing me in.

He was still smiling. Either he or his parents had spent a fortune on his teeth. "Your husband said you might have something to tell us about what went on over here at the motel."

I reminded myself that my first goal was to talk to Joe. "Where is Joe?"

"He's cooperating with the investigation."

"I'd like to see him."

"It will be a while before he's free."

"I can wait."

"He said he'd told you to be ready to make a statement. So why not tell me what went down?" Detective Robertson's smile became even more friendly, and I was getting lots of eye contact. Was he trying to flirt with me? Surely not.

I tried to speak in a friendly manner. "I'd like to understand the simulation—I mean, the situation! I'd like to understand what's going on before I do make a statistic. I mean, a statement!"

Yikes! I'd gotten my tongue in a double twist. No matter what I told the detective now, he wasn't going to think I was smart enough to know what I was talking about.

My malapropisms made Detective Robertson give a bigger grin. "I thought you and I could talk informally."

I tried to recover my dignity. "I assume y'all have the witnesses over at the motel."

"Y'all?" Robertson smiled even more widely. My Texas accent had been the final flourish to convince him that I was some backward Southern belle who couldn't think straight. "Y'all jes tell Uncle Van all about it." He leaned closer to me, displaying his eyeteeth.

He shouldn't have done that. Those teeth reminded me strongly of Dr. Fletcher Mendenhall, and I gave an involuntary shudder. "No!"

"Honey chile! I can be a very friendly guy."

"We're not friends, Detective Robertson. We're doing business—your business. I want to talk to my husband before I say anything else."

"Honey, your husband could be in big trouble. If you're so concerned about him, you'd better tell me what happened."

"I'll be glad to make a statement, but my husband is the attorney in the family, and I don't feel I can do that until I consult him."

"All we want 'y'all' to do is tell us the truth."

"Then let me talk to my husband."

"You could save him a lot of trouble by talking to me now, honey." He was still grinning, and I could swear he had edged closer to me.

I reached into my purse and took out a notebook. "Let me be sure I'm spelling your name correctly," I said. "Was your first name Van? V-A-N?"

Robertson backed off slightly. "Yes."

"And is your last name Robertson? Not Robinson?"

Now he was frowning. "Robertson."

"And what is your badge number?"

"You don't need that."

"Probably not. But it might help, in case I decide to file a complaint."

"You don't have any grounds for a complaint."

"Don't I? You have made fun of my state of origin—and believe me, Detective Robertson, that's not something Texans take lightly." I allowed myself a small smile. "You have called me 'Honey chile' and 'Honey' on three occasions, and I consider that harassment."

"Lady . . ."

"And you have refused to take me to the area where witnesses are being questioned. I consider that you have behaved in a most unprofessional manner. Of course, before making a final judgment I will consult my uncle, who is a police chief with thirty years' experience on the Cincinnati police force."

He frowned, and I fired one final shot. "And please get out of my side of this booth. I don't like feeling that you're trapping me inside it."

He slid out, his face like a Texas thundercloud, and gestured. "You want to join the other witnesses? Come along."

As I stood up, I was delighted to realize that I was two inches taller than he was. Actually, I was probably his height, but by some bit of luck I'd picked the boots with three-inch heels to wear that day. I threw my shoulders back and looked down at him, then walked toward the front of the restaurant.

Part of me realized that ticking off a detective wasn't smart. It might even get me arrested. But after the condescending way he'd acted, I enjoyed myself all the way to the cashier. And I refused to allow him to pay for my coffee.

I stayed on my high horse as I walked to the motel, stepping through the snow as if I were grinding my heels into Robertson's face with every step. But even after we got to the motel, I didn't see Joe. As star witness, I realized, he was probably being kept in solitary confinement someplace. I was marched into the motel lobby and told to be seated in the tiny area with chairs, tables, and a television set. Two giant hot pots and a selection of plastic-wrapped pastries were on a shelf along one side, so I deduced that the motel offered a continental breakfast.

"Don't talk to anyone," Robertson said. He left through a back door, but a uniformed patrolman was sitting with us. I didn't know if he was there to enforce the no-talking edict or to listen in if any of us felt compelled to confess.

There were only two other people present, two women. Both of them wore smocks with their names over the pockets. Both looked Hispanic. Having been told not to talk, I immediately felt the urge to trot out my high school Spanish, but I resisted. I also resisted the temptation to have a cup of the motel's coffee, which had probably been stewing since six a.m. I took off my coat, and I simply sat. One of the women had been crying, and I didn't like to stare at her, so I stared at the floor.

I was still staring at the floor—the carpet was patterned with blue amoebas and was none too clean—when a figure sat down next to me. I looked up, hoping it was Joe, but no such luck.

It was a young kid, wearing a white shirt and black tie. He wore his hair slicked back, and he'd used too much hair gel. He leaned toward me and spoke in a low voice. "Hey. I could help you out."

I didn't answer. After all, I'd been told not to talk. Instead I looked for the uniformed cop who'd been sitting with us. He was gone.

"I could help you," the young man said again. "And you could return the favor."

"I don't think I need help, thank you," I said. "And we were told not to talk."

"The cops are going to ask me to identify the woman who dropped the dead guy off yesterday. But I could forget what she looked like."

I stood up and moved to a chair across the room.

The young guy shrugged, then got to his feet. He walked through a door at the other end of the lobby and immediately reappeared behind the reception desk. He picked up a telephone and spoke into it. His voice was loud.

"Yeah, she's the one," he said.

I was getting madder by the minute. Somebody was using cheap tricks to put me on the defensive. I didn't know if it was the cheesy desk clerk or the cheesy detective, but I wasn't feeling defensive. I was, as a matter of fact, ready to go on the offensive.

So as soon as the uniformed cop came back, I confronted him. "Who's in charge here?"

"Sergeant McCullough. He'll be out soon."

"I hope so. I'm getting sick of being harassed."

The cop I was talking to merely scowled, but a sympathetic voice came from behind me. "Harassed? We can't have that."

I turned, and all I saw was Joe. Without a word, I threw my arms around him.

Joe chuckled. "Hey! It's okay."

"Why wouldn't they let me see you?"

"They don't want us to give each other hints about what to say, Lee."

"Now, Mr. Woodyard . . ." The words came from a fatherly-looking man with beautiful white hair and a matching white mustache. He smiled beneficently. "Your husband has been very cooperative, Mrs. Woodyard. Now if you'll just give us your statement, I'm sure this matter can be cleared up."

He was completely reassuring, the personification of kindness and understanding. I could feel myself begin to relax.

Joe spoke then. "This is Sergeant McCullough, Lee. Just tell him the absolute truth. Strictly factual."

Joe sounded as reassuring as McCullough looked. The only hitch was that he squeezed my hand really hard at the same time he was talking. Then he turned his head so that the detective couldn't see his face, and he gave me a direct, hard look. And that squeeze and that look both said, "Watch out!"

I squeezed his hand back. "I'll be glad to make a statement, Joe, though I have no idea what happened to Mendenhall. But I'd appreciate your staying with me."

"It's probably best if I don't," Joe said. "If you're uneasy, I can call Webb Bartlett."

McCullough chuckled. "Oh, it doesn't sound as if Mrs. Woodyard will need an attorney."

"Webb and I were in law school together," Joe said. He was being chummy with McCullough. "Lee knows him as a friend."

Webb had represented my ex-husband's son a couple of years earlier, when the teenager was suspected—falsely—in a Warner Pier crime. Joe and I occasionally went out to dinner with Webb and his wife, and they'd come to our wedding. Yes, I considered Webb a friend.

"I'll wait for you here," Joe said. He smiled as if that was his idea, but I felt sure that McCullough wouldn't allow him to leave until he made sure our statements matched. I just hoped he'd let both of us leave after we'd told all.

McCullough, talking about the weather, escorted me to a room just down the hall. It was a regular motel room, but it did have a table and chairs crammed into one end. I didn't have to sit on the bed. Detective Robertson did.

McCullough smiled, looking like a benevolent grand-daddy. "Now, Mrs. Woodyard, how did you happen to pick Dr. Mendenhall up at the airport?"

I told the whole story, trying to keep it brief. McCullough didn't interrupt me. I made it through with only a few slips of the tongue, ending with Mendenhall running after me as I drove off.

McCullough was still smiling. "So, you led Mendenhall to believe that you would go to this motel room with him."

"I tried not to say or do anything that would imply that."

"But he thought you would be coming in."

"Not from anything I said. I said, 'If you feel this way, you need to get a room.' I did not say, 'We need to get a room.' I was careful to say 'you.' I never—never—told him I would be joining him in it."

"But you let him think you would be coming in."

"What he thought was not my responsibility, Sergeant McCullough. Anyway, the prospect scared him spitless."

"It scared him?"

"Yes. You know, these types who come on so hard don't really want to succeed." I couldn't resist taking a look at Detective Robertson. "He simply wanted to embarrass me."

"And did he?"

"Of course. Ask your wife. An episode like that is extremely embarrassing to any woman. But it also made me mad."

"Mad enough to hit him?"

"Mad enough to shove him back onto his own side of the seat when he started breathing down my neck. But my main object was simply to get rid of him. I didn't want to drive forty-five more minutes—in heavy traffic on winter roads—trying to fend him off. For one thing, I probably would have had a wreck."

"You came up with an ingenious way to get rid of him, Mrs. Woodyard." He chuckled and turned to Robertson. "Ask Mr. Woodyard to step in."

He hummed softly while we waited for Joe, and he greeted him with a broad smile. I was beginning to relax. Maybe we'd be able to leave right away.

Joe dropped a hand on my shoulder as he came in. He stood behind me, and we both looked at McCullough.

The detective smiled his beneficent smile again. "Now," he said, "if I could just decide which one of you I ought to charge."

Really Ancient Chocolate

Among the big anthropological news of the early 2000s was a report that scientists had proved use of chocolate by humankind began five hundred years earlier than previously thought.

An analysis of ancient pottery from Honduras found traces of chocolate at least three thousand years old. This is five hundred years earlier than any earlier evidence of the use of the heavenly substance.

A professor of anthropology at Cornell University, John Henderson, and his colleagues made chemical analyses of residue on bits of broken pottery dating from 1100 B.C., pottery found in the Ulua Valley of northern Honduras. The scientists discovered theobroma, an alkaloid present only in cacao.

Scientists speculate that the vessels had been used to drink a fermented "beer" made from the pulp that surrounds the cacao beans used to produce chocolate.

The pottery was of a type used for important ceremonies, the researchers said.

Chapter 5

Joe pulled his phone from his pocket. "I've got Webb Bartlett on my cell," he said. "Should I call?"

"Aw, I don't think you need a lawyer yet," McCullough said. "It's just that there are so many ways to interpret your stories."

"So what's to interpret?" Joe said. "I told you the truth, and I'm sure Lee did, too."

"Your stories match—that's for sure." The detective smiled his kindly smile. "Of course, you had all night to match 'em up. But Mrs. Woodyard might have gone into that motel room to put Mendenhall's bag down, and he could have tried to assault her. She would have been perfectly justified in crowning him with the desk lamp."

"But if I was perfectly justified, wouldn't the smart thing have been to call the cops as soon as he hit the floor?" I said. "Get my story in first?"

McCullough nodded. "Yep. And you're obviously a smart lady. But even smart people can panic. Or you might not have realized how bad he was hurt."

"Since he was hopping up and down like Rumpelstiltskin when I drove off, that scenery—I mean, scenario! That scenario doesn't apply."

Joe spoke. "On the other hand, when Lee told me Mendenhall had gotten fresh with her, I might have been so mad I came by here and had some sort of confrontation with him, ending with using the desk lamp as a bludgeon."

"No, Joe," I said. "That won't work either. You were a wrestler."

McCullough looked confused. "A wrestler?"

"Right," I said. "Joe was state wrestling champ for one hundred seventy-five pounds the year he was a senior in high school. I was present a couple of years ago when one of the local nutcases down at Warner Pier took a poke at him. Joe did not punch him back. That wrestling training kicked in, and Joe had the guy in a headlock in less than a second. Pure instinct. He wouldn't have needed a table lamp to handle Mendenhall."

Joe snorted. "Thanks, Lee. You're saying I would never have hit Mendenhall. I would have simply broken his neck."

McCullough laughed.

Joe went on. "Neither of us had any reason to kill Mendenhall deliberately, and neither of us is the kind to get mad enough to do it. And if either of us hit him in self-defense, we're both smart enough to call the police immediately and tell our side."

McCullough grinned. "You're talking like a defense attorney, Joe."

"Yep."

"I bet you're a heck of a cross-examiner," the detective said. "Now, if you'll both go down to the station, you can make formal statements. Plus, we'll have to get your fingerprints."

"Of course," I said. "I know you have to make sure neither of us left any prints in the room."

"You weren't in there at all?"

"No. I handled Mendenhall's suitcase, as I said. And his flask. And the box of TenHuis chocolates. I don't remember if

I had my gloves on or not. But I don't see how my fingerprints could be on any other item in that room."

"And I never got inside," Joe said. "I could hear Mendenhall's cell phone ring, but he didn't come to the door."

"Cell phone." McCullough sounded thoughtful. "What kind of cell phone did Mendenhall have?"

"I never saw it," I said. "I talked to him on it, but he had put it away by the time we met at the airport."

"I only heard it," Joe said. "Or I guess I did. I called his number from outside the room, and I could hear the 'Hallelujah Chorus.' But he didn't answer, and I never saw Mendenhall at all. Alive."

"You heard the 'Hallelujah Chorus'?"

"That's right. One of those special rings."

McCullough made just one more request before he sent Joe and me off to headquarters. He asked to search my purse.

I responded by dumping the contents out on the bed, then handing the empty bag to McCullough. He and Robertson looked through my junk. I had makeup, keys, a billfold—containing an embarrassingly small amount of money, two credit cards, and a snapshot of Joe—two old grocery lists, a packet of Kleenex, and a small zipper case with a dozen plastic cards which entitled me to special treatment when buying books, groceries, greeting cards, hardware, and other items. They looked at all the numbers in my cell phone and wrote down the one I said belonged to Mendenhall.

Joe and I were then driven to the Lake Knapp police station. We each had another session, going over our stories. Mine didn't change, and I'm sure Joe's didn't either. Then we each had our fingerprints taken with one of those strange electronic machines now in use for that chore. It was two hours before we were delivered back to the motel. By then it was way past lunchtime. Joe moved his truck to the parking lot of the chain restaurant next door, and we went in and grabbed a booth.

I ordered a hamburger with extra mustard and pickles and told them to leave everything else off; Michigan has great food, but ordinary, everyday restaurants tend to think a hamburger is a dry meat patty and a dry bun. If they put anything on, it's ketchup, and that's heresy to a Texan.

As soon as the waitress left, I spoke to Joe. "Did I see traces of fingerprint dust on your dashboard?"

"Yep. I told them to go ahead and search the truck. I guess they didn't find anything, or they would have kept it."

"Do you think McCullough seriously suspects either of us?"

"He seems to be a pretty smart guy, Lee, so I imagine that he's still keeping all his options open. I can see at least one thing that doesn't seem to fit in with either of us killing Mendenhall."

"What's that?"

"The guy's cell phone is missing."

I gasped. "Golly! That went right by me."

"Yeah. McCullough didn't make a big deal out of it, but it's obvious that they haven't found Mendenhall's cell phone."

"It could still turn up in the motel room. Under the bed or someplace."

"By now they will have looked every place that's likely. My guess is that the killer took it."

"Why?"

The waitress came with our drinks then, so I had time to think through the answer to my own question. As soon as she left, Joe and I leaned toward each other and did our unison-speaking act again.

"The killer's number was on the phone." Then we both sat back, looking at each other.

"But, Joe," I said, "can't the police trace Mendenhall's calls, even without the phone?"

"Sure. The cops will find out who had his phone service

and call them. They'll know all the calls he made—oh, by five o'clock today—even if they don't find the phone."

"Then why would the killer take it away?"

"Maybe he—or she—took it by accident. That's one reason they searched the truck. Mendenhall could have dropped it there. And it might have somehow wound up in your purse."

"Like he left it in the seat of the truck, and I thought it was mine? Something like that." I grabbed up my ski jacket and hastily went though the pockets. "No, I'm sure I don't have it. I was wearing jeans yesterday, and they're tight. I would never have put a cell phone in my pants pocket."

"I know you don't have it," Joe said, "because when I called Mendenhall's cell number around six thirty yesterday, I heard the phone ring inside the room. But when I called this morning, standing outside his door, I didn't hear it. So I think that phone left the premises between last night and this morning."

"But taking the phone was useless, since the cops can trace the calls anyway."

Joe shrugged. "The killer might not have known that."

"You mean it's someone who doesn't know much about phones?"

"Could be."

"But who would Mendenhall have called? George didn't talk as if the man had any personal connection with Michigan."

"He'd been in contact with George, of course. But in any case, McCullough and his team will figure it out."

"I guess there's nothing we can do."

Joe reached across the table and took my hand. "There's one thing I can do, Lee. Warn you about McCullough."

"I caught on to the fatherly act."

"Good. I did call Webb while they were questioning you. Just to alert him to the situation."

"What was his advice?"

"Play it just the way we have been. Be honest and open. But he said not to underestimate McCullough. He retired from the Grand Rapids force—and Webb was a little cagey about that."

"McCullough retired under a cloud?"

"Webb wouldn't say. McCullough's record wasn't bad enough to keep this suburban force from hiring him. But Webb says McCullough's a really smart guy and can be tricky. So if he wants to question you again, call Webb before you talk to him. Okay?"

I shuddered. "I hate this, Joe. I hate having to watch every word I say. I hate being under suspicion. I hate having people think I'm capable of killing someone."

At that point I looked up and my eyes met those of the man in the next booth. He was staring right at me, and I couldn't believe the look on his face. It could only be called a leer.

A stranger was leering at me? Why? I was dressed conservatively—blazer and slacks. I wasn't wearing a lot of makeup. And I thought I'd been behaving myself.

Then I recognized the guy. It was the desk clerk from the motel, the one who had offered to "do me a favor," apparently meaning he would not identify me as the woman who dropped Mendenhall off at the motel. He hadn't specified what favor I would have had to do in return. But he'd made it clear he had thought I was a professional girl bringing a client to his motel.

The creep.

"I also hate people thinking I'm a call girl," I said.

Joe's eyes popped. "Who thinks that?"

"The guy in the booth behind you." We hadn't been talking loudly, but I lowered my voice even more as I told Joe about my run-in with the desk clerk.

Joe frowned. He also kept his voice low. "It would give me a lot of pleasure to tie him in a knot," he said. "But right at this juncture it probably wouldn't be a good idea to do the protective-husband act."

"I'm afraid McCullough would be sure to hear about it," I said. "You'd probably be in jail before the hamburgers get here. Let's talk about something else. For example, I stopped by George Jenkins' gallery this morning and told him he'd lost another juror."

We talked about George, then went on to the rest of the WinterFest committee.

"Do you think we need to call Ramona?" I said.

"Let George do it. I'm hungry."

The food came, and we both tucked in. As I predicted, the hamburgers weren't much, but the French fries were pretty good, and there was a tomato slice on the side of the plate. We ate in a hurry, since we both wanted to get out of there and head home. The desk clerk in the next booth had just received his order when we stood up, ready to go.

Joe winked at me and spoke loudly. "You'll have to hurry, dear. I know you don't want to be late for Bible study."

I tried not to look at the desk clerk, but his eyes were wide as we went by his booth. I didn't laugh.

The day had warmed up, and the gutters of the busy street were full of slush, so Joe drove me across the street, left me at my van, then told me he'd see me at home. While the van was warming up, I called Aunt Nettie, to tell her I was okay and to see how TenHuis Chocolade was going. I think I wanted to touch base with my normal life.

"Oh, Lee, I've been so worried," she said. "Does Hogan need to come up there and see what's going on? I mean, what's the point of having a police chief in the family if you never use him?"

I assured Aunt Nettie that Joe and I were on our way

home, but I didn't tell her we were both still under suspicion. We could discuss the situation with Hogan later.

Hogan Jones and his first wife had moved to Warner Pier after he had retired from the Cincinnati police department. After his wife died the next year, he became the chief and the sole detective for Warner Pier's five-person police department. And the previous summer he'd taken on Aunt Nettie as the second Mrs. Jones. Both of them had had long, happy first marriages, and they seemed to be settling in for a second marriage that would be as happy and maybe as long.

Aunt Nettie did pass along two messages: Ramona VanWinkle-Snow and George Jenkins both wanted me to call as soon as possible. I sighed. I knew these were the first of many calls from people who would want all the details on Mendenhall.

I started with George, since Aunt Nettie said he had called first. He answered on the second ring.

"Hi," I said. "It's Lee. Were you able to get the show judged?"

"Oh, yes, that worked out." Then George began to ask about just what had happened, but I said I'd talk to him later. "I need to get started for home," I said, "and I don't like to talk while I'm driving if I can avoid it."

"I just wish I'd had my phone turned on last night so I could take Mendenhall's call."

"I'd forgotten that you said Mendenhall called you last night. That call may be important!"

"It wasn't important enough for him to tell me what he wanted. He just made some incoherent remarks and left his number."

I started to tell George that Mendenhall's phone was missing, then decided to allow McCullough to handle that. After all, I might be mistaken.

"Phone calls Mendenhall made to anyone might be important," I said. "I wouldn't erase the message."

"I had e-mailed Mendenhall a copy of the committee roster," George said. "He could have called anybody."

I hung up then and sat in the supermarket parking lot, thinking a moment, before I called Ramona. Mendenhall had had a complete list of the WinterFest committee members. Hmmm.

I pictured Mendenhall running down the sidewalk as I pulled out of the motel. He'd been furious. So, I wondered, after I disappeared, what would he have done?

A man that mad probably wouldn't just go back to his room and watch television, I decided. No, he'd do something, even if it was stupid. And since we knew he had a cell phone, and we could assume he'd brought his list of WinterFest committee members with him, and he was unlikely to know anybody else in Michigan—well, he probably got that list out and began calling people.

I had just reached that conclusion when the phone in my hand rang. It did not play "The Hallelujah Chorus," but I jumped as if the noise was the last trumpet. I probably sounded scared to death when I answered. "Hello."

"Lee, it's Ramona."

"I just got your message."

"Are you and Joe all right? Will you be back soon?"

"Yes. We had to make statements, and it took a lot of time, but I'm leaving Grand Rapids now."

"We've called a special committee meeting for six thirty. I hope both of you can make it. It will be at the Warner Point Center office, right before the opening reception."

The opening reception. Damn. After the day I'd had so far, the last thing I wanted to do was go to a big party where everybody I knew was going to want Joe and me to tell them all the details about finding a murdered man and explain how

Fletcher Mendenhall came to be in the place where he was found.

My impulse was to tell Ramona I was going to go home, take a hot shower, and crawl in bed.

But logic asserted itself.

First, Joe and I simply couldn't hole up and refuse to see our friends. It might make us look guilty.

Second, if we went to the meeting and the party, the whole WinterFest committee ought to be there. Maybe we would find out more about Mendenhall and whether he had called anybody with the missing phone.

"Joe and I might be a bit late," I said, "but we'll be there."

Chapter 6

I got to the office at four o'clock and found a dozen e-mails waiting. I replied to one of them—a major customer who needed a rush order of eight-inch chocolate Christmas trees decorated with tiny chocolate toys. I promised that we'd make them the next day and overnight them to her. The rest of the messages dealt with Valentine's Day items or chocolates from our regular stock. They could wait, but it was still after five when I left for home to get ready for the WinterFest art show opening reception, the biggest event of Warner Pier's limited winter social season.

I'd called Joe as soon as I talked to Ramona, so he'd gone straight home and was already getting dressed when I got there. I jumped into our wonderful tiled shower and felt glad Joe had remodeled the old farmhouse bathroom as soon as we had moved in the previous summer. When I got out I was ready to climb into my best party dress—the knee-length champagne number I'd worn to get married the previous spring. It had long sleeves, so I could wear it around the calendar. I did drape a paisley shawl over my shoulders. The gold, brown, rust, and amber shades complemented the dress, I thought, and would make me look wintry. Joe was wearing his wedding outfit, too, though probably I was the only person who could tell it wasn't his regular lawyer suit. By six fifteen we were ready to knock 'em dead at the WinterFest opening.

Before we went out the door, I asked Joe a question. "Do we have any goal at this event?"

"Goal?"

"Yes. You're city attorney. You often need to drop a casual word to someone, something you want to say without making it look purposeful. I've known you to leave for the post office at seven in the morning so you could catch somebody 'accidentally.' "

"True."

"So? What about tonight? Do we have a goal?"

"I always have people I need to talk to about city business. But as far as a goal for you and me, it's to let it be known that the Lake Knapp police want to talk to anybody who spoke with Mendenhall last night."

"And to tell everybody we didn't do him in."

"Right."

"And to come home early. I'm exhausted."

"Right again." Joe kissed my cheek. "Let's go."

We got into the van and drove to the Warner Point Conference Center.

The conference center has played an important part in our lives. Ten years earlier, the land it stood on had been acquired by Joe's first wife, famed defense attorney Clementine Ripley, as payment for a legal fee. The triangular property has Lake Michigan as one boundary and the Warner River as a second. All that waterfront makes it one of the most valuable pieces of property within a hundred miles.

On it Clementine Ripley built a showplace home, actually a series of stone buildings, simple in design and linked by glassed-in walkways. Then she stained the woodwork and floors stark black, and had the walls painted stark white. The result, to my way of thinking, was rooms that looked so cold they were like walk-in freezers even when the temperature was ninety degrees outside.

Joe never talks much about his life as Clementine Ripley's husband, but he did tell me she didn't consult him about the house. Or maybe he didn't show any interest when he *was* consulted. Anyhow, he only admits having input on the boathouse.

The house seems to have been one of the final nails in the coffin of the Woodyard-Ripley marriage. Joe hated it, and he was beginning to realize that his original feelings for his wife had been based on a sort of crazy hero-worship, an admiration for her abilities as a defense attorney, rather than a true estimate of her character. At the same time Clementine was apparently realizing the young lawyer she had married wasn't willing to approve her questionable ethics and didn't like her spend-like-there's-no-tomorrow lifestyle. The divorce was amicable in the sense that they both wanted out.

A year later Clementine died without changing a will made while she and Joe were married, and Joe discovered that he had inherited her estate—including the Warner Point house. The inheritance only added to the nightmare the marriage had been; Joe immediately made it known he didn't want her money. Then he discovered the truth—there *was* very little money. The Warner Point house and Clementine's apartment in Chicago were heavily mortgaged, and an adviser Clementine had trusted had made off with most of her investments. It took Joe two years to get the estate straightened out, and it took two years and all the money he could get together to pay off the Warner Point property's mortgage.

And as soon as he'd done that, Joe gave the property to the Village of Warner Pier, to be used as a conference center. He couldn't do it anonymously, since everybody knew who owned it, but he declined any public recognition of his gift.

Now the property was gradually becoming useful to the

city. Jason Foster had leased the main building and opened a snazzy restaurant, including rooms for special events. It was drawing weddings and smaller banquets from all over western Michigan. An experienced bed-and-breakfast operator was about to build an adjoining inn. There was talk of putting up an outdoor pavilion for summer events.

And Joe was gradually becoming able to enter the property without visibly shuddering.

He dropped me at the wide stone steps leading to the main entrance, since they had been thoroughly cleared of snow. Even the giant snowman was gone for the evening; a volunteer would be wearing the suit for the art show opening. But the building looked festive, with swags of greenery, tiny lights, and red bows everywhere.

The minute the front door swung open, I was ambushed by Johnny Owens.

He grabbed my shoulders with both hands. "Lee! I feel terrible! It never occurred to me that you would go to pick Mendenhall up! I'm so sorry I let you get into this mess!"

"You let me? Johnny, you had nothing to do with it."

Johnny let go of my shoulders and ran his hands through his buzz cut. "If I'd had any idea in the world that Joe would have to ask you to make the airport run . . ."

I was beginning to see what Johnny was talking about. "Then you knew that Mendenhall had a problem with inappropriate behavior toward women?"

"Not firsthand! I mean, I never witnessed him doing anything wrong. It's just that—well, there was always a lot of gossip about him."

"Do you mean when you were in college?" I said.

"Yeah. I've been out of school fifteen years. But if one of the women on the committee had volunteered to pick him up, believe me, I would have said something. When Joe said he'd do it, I thought it was the ideal situation."

"I don't see how you can blame yourself, Johnny. The whole thing would probably have been okay if Mendenhall hadn't been drinking."

"Drinking? I didn't know he'd become a drinker." Johnny grimaced. "His reputation for coming on to women—including students—was bad. But I'd never heard he drank."

"A lot can change in fifteen years. Anyway, I dropped him at the motel as soon as I realized that he was pretty polluted. I don't know what happened to him later. His death is a complete mystery to me."

Joe walked in at that point, and Johnny went into a new spasm of self-reproach and apology. Joe was gracious, but his voice had a brusque edge.

"I don't see how you could have anticipated my passing off the pickup chore to Lee," he said. "And we're certainly not holding you responsible for Mendenhall's bad behavior. But I would have appreciated a hint."

"That's what I'm kicking myself about," Johnny said. "But it's awful hard to hint when all you have to go on is gossip."

"I have one big question," I said. "What makes a guy like that think he's attractive to women?"

"I guess he remembers his glory days."

"Glory days!" I'm sure I sounded as astonished as I felt. "Are you saying Mendenhall once *was* attractive to women?"

"That was the story."

"It wasn't because of his appearance. A short, fat, bald guy has a lot to overcome."

"Mendenhall got fat? And he lost his hair?"

"I didn't see a photo ID, but the fellow I met at the airport was fat and bald."

"He used to be fairly good-looking, certainly not fat. And he had a great head of hair. The gossip was that he was very attractive to women."

"Women like Mrs. Trustee?"

"Not just her. There was one story . . ." Johnny's voice trailed off, and I realized he was blushing.

"It was just a story," he said weakly.

His reaction was almost amusing. I leaned close and lowered my voice. "Orgies?"

Johnny's cheeks became slightly redder. "I'm not sure how you define an orgy," he said. "How many people does it take?"

"I suppose it depends on what they're doing," Joe said. "Come on, Lee. Ramona's beckoning us into the meeting. You'll have to wait for the salacious details."

The three of us went into the WinterFest office to find Ramona and George Jenkins already there. George rushed to meet us.

"Oh, Lee, Joe! You two have had a terrible time! I'm so sorry!"

"It wasn't your fault, George," I said. "What have you done about a juror?"

"That worked out. I went to Dr. Harrison. And in the emergency, he agreed to serve."

"Who is Dr. Harrison?"

"I thought everyone knew him! He's one of our most famous residents."

"Sorry, George. I know nothing about art."

"Dr. Thomas Harrison was head of the art department at the University of Michigan. He retired here in Warner Pier. His wife is in poor health, and they live a very quiet life. He doesn't take part in community activities. But in the current emergency, he agreed to step in." George cleared his throat. "Of course, a juror really ought to be from outside the local area, someone who wouldn't know any of the hometown artists. But since Dr. Harrison isn't active in Warner Pier art circles, and since he's so well-known and respected, and since it's a real emergency—I don't think anyone will complain."

I sighed. "That's a relief. It sounds as if you handled the situation very well."

Ramona spoke briskly. "We'll have to discuss paying Dr. Harrison a fee, Lee. That's part of the business we need to handle now."

George nodded. "And everyone will want to know about what happened. We heard the most awful rumors. One was that you two were questioned by the Grand Rapids police."

"It was the Lake Knapp police," Joe said. "And I know everyone's going to want to hear all about it. Let's wait until the crowd is here."

So we all sat down and looked at one another. When we all had only one subject on our minds, and we'd agreed not to talk about it—well, it sure killed other conversation.

Then I gasped. Mozelle had walked in.

Ramona greeted her with apparent pleasure. "You're here!"

"Luckily, I was able to conclude my business and come back for the WinterFest opening," Mozelle said. "I should be here for all the events."

We all assured her we were delighted that her plans had changed. I told myself I wasn't being hypocritical; I might not like Mozelle, but she was doing a good job for the WinterFest.

The rest of the committee trickled in. Each wore a personal version of dress-up clothes. Sarajane Harding had on a neat navy blue pantsuit, rather tailored, but obviously not expensive, and had brought her dimples and straight gray hair. George had replaced his usual tweed jacket with a burgundy blazer, but he still wore a turtleneck. Mary Samson was in something short and floaty that made me wonder if she'd bought it for her high school prom. Then I wondered if our shy Mary had even gone to the high school prom.

Ramona had something black, bulky, and ankle-length, with a multi-multi-multicolored velvet scarf draped around her neck. Johnny Owens wore jeans and a flannel shirt, his usual garb, but I could tell it was dress-up because he wasn't smeared with clay or paint. Maggie McNutt, who knew exactly what was becoming for her tiny frame, was stylish in red taffeta.

Mozelle was dressed in basic black, which had probably cost more than the total of all the other garments in the room. It wasn't exciting, but it sure was cut well.

A few minutes later Amos Hart arrived. He wore his usual bow tie, but this one was black and almost made him look as if he were in a tuxedo.

Most of these people tried to talk to Joe and me, but Ramona sternly motioned everyone into chairs around the meeting table. "So, can we now have an official report on what in the world happened to Mendenhall?"

I deferred to Joe, as the one of us who would know how to avoid saying more than we should, and he outlined the events of the previous evening and the current day.

He ended by saying, "I think all of you can expect to hear from the Lake Knapp police. They'll want to know if Mendenhall tried to contact any of you."

"He didn't call me," Maggie McNutt said. "I didn't have anything to do with the art show. And how would he have known that I even existed?"

George broke in to explain that he'd e-mailed Mendenhall a packet of information on the Winter Festival, and in it had been a list of the organizing committee members.

Maggie frowned. "Actually, I wasn't available last night, since I was at rehearsal. I had my cell phone turned off, and both Ken and I were at the auditorium from six o'clock on. I'll check my answering machine, but I didn't notice it flashing."

"George and I were at his gallery during the early part of the evening," Ramona said with a slight smile. "We were handling a last-minute crisis with the art show, and I had my phone turned off, too. Later I was home, but Mendenhall didn't call. Bob didn't mention getting any calls earlier."

"Anyone who got a call from Mendenhall would probably be wise to call the Lake Knapp police and ask for Sergeant McCullough," Joe said.

"Oh, dear." Mary Samson's voice was almost a whimper. "Would we have to?"

"It would be a good idea, Mary. Did Mendenhall call you?"

Mary wrung her hands. "Someone did. Someone who sounded drunk. I thought it was a crank call."

"That may have been Mendenhall," I said. "He was certainly drunk when I left him."

"He didn't make any sense," Mary said. "I couldn't repeat anything he said to the police. I—well, I hung up on him."

"Still," Joe said, "they'll want to know what he said."

"But he didn't say anything! I mean, anything that made sense. Are you sure I need to call this detective?"

"It would look better if you called McCullough before he called you."

"But why would he try to contact me? How would he even know Mendenhall had called me? I mean, just because I was on the list."

Joe explained about phone records being readily available to investigators. "So I'm sorry, Mary. But the police will have your number, and they'll want to know what Mendenhall had to say."

Ramona broke off the discussion.

"We'd better drop this," she said. "George found an excellent juror to take Mendenhall's place, and we need to approve paying him."

George then repeated his story about getting the cooperation of Dr. Thomas Harrison. All the artists looked properly impressed. Then George turned to Ramona. "But Dr. Harrison said he would decline payment for his service."

Everyone murmured at that, but I spoke up. "We should refuse his offer, George."

"But why? We need the money."

"True. But we want to do things in a professional way. I would suggest that we go ahead and approve paying his fee. Then, if he wants, he can make a donation of an equal amount to the festival. That way he can receive a tax deduction for the donation. I don't think our fee is large enough to cause him an income tax problem."

The committee approved that plan, and the meeting adjourned. As it did, I realized that it had been remarkable for one thing.

Mozelle had been there, and she hadn't said a word.

Chapter 7

The idea of Mozelle being at a meeting and not saying anything was so surprising that for a moment I thought she must have left. I quickly looked around the room. There was Mozelle. Yes, she had attended the whole meeting, and, no, she hadn't said anything.

Odd. It was hard to believe that Mozelle hadn't felt compelled to add to the discussion. Mozelle always talked, whether she had anything useful to say or not.

I was still mulling this over when Joe leaned over and spoke into my ear. He said he wanted to catch his mother as soon as she came in, to reassure her that neither of us had been given the third degree by the Lake Knapp police. He left me still considering Mozelle's unexpected silence. By the time I had slung my shawl around my shoulders, I decided Mozelle's actions were not my prime consideration that evening, and I was ready to join the art show opening. But when I left the WinterFest office, Mozelle popped up in front of me so suddenly I jumped as if I'd stepped on a snake.

"You've certainly had an interesting twenty-four hours," she said.

"A little too interesting."

"Mendenhall—did he say anything to you about having a Michigan connection?"

"No, Mozelle. I understood from George that it was important for a juror not to know the artists in our region."

"Oh, he might not know the artists personally. But if people enter art shows around the country, he might be familiar with their work."

"If he was, he didn't mention it. But we only exchanged a few words."

"He might have forgotten."

"Might have forgotten what?"

"Whom, Lee. Not what."

I finally saw that Mozelle was giving me a hint. "Oh," I said, "did you know him?"

"Oh, no!" Her voice was horrified. "No, no! Not me."

"Then whom are you talking about?"

"I'd prefer not to say. And I wasn't present when this alleged episode occurred." Mozelle looked around, apparently checking to see who was standing behind her. "I heard that a local artist was in a show Mendenhall judged several years ago. The artist didn't like the way the judging went. The two of them supposedly exchanged words." She leaned forward and lowered her voice. "Then they exchanged punches."

"You'd better tell the police about this," I said.

"Do you think so?" Her voice was slyer than ever.

My reaction was a desire to exchange a punch or two myself. With Mozelle. She was trying to get some Warner Pier artist in trouble.

"If Mendenhall had an enemy here, Mozelle, the police need that information."

"I'd really prefer not to get involved."

"I'm afraid you will be, like it or not. The police will be calling everyone whose name was on that list of committee members."

Mozelle smiled her sly smile again. "Then they won't be contacting me. I'm not on that list."

"You're not?"

"If it's the list in the WinterFest brochure, the ex officio members were not listed. Mayor Herrera and I were omitted."

She turned and left the room, still smiling.

I followed her into the reception room. I was seething—Mozelle always had that effect on me—but I tried to look pleasant.

When Jason Foster had remodeled the main Warner Point house into a restaurant, he'd warmed it up a lot from Clementine Ripley's original decor. For one thing, he covered the big windows with deep red draperies, so we were not staring out into the winter darkness.

I walked past the main dining room, where the tables wore white cloths and were centered with jewel-toned lamps surrounded by seasonal greenery dotted with shiny golden balls. Then I went across the entry hall and toward the east end of the building. The art show was set up in a large room Jason used for private dinners and receptions. It had once been Clementine Ripley's five-car garage.

Screens and special lighting had turned the area into a labyrinth. Pieces of sculpture were dotted here and there, including a large metal reindeer created by Johnny Owens. A mobile hung overhead. The bar and the main food service table were in an anteroom. Already the area was filling with art lovers; Warner Pier's winter population may be only 2,500, but it seems that at least half are artists or gallery owners. Plus, the Warner Pier Winter Festival Art Show had begun attracting art fans from Holland, from Kalamazoo, from Grand Rapids, and from the other art colonies scattered up and down the shore of Lake Michigan. I recognized people from Saugatuck and from South Haven.

When I got to the food room, which was decorated with greenery and golden ornaments coordinating with the restaurant dining room, I was just in time to see Aunt Nettie receive a round of applause. She had unveiled the centerpiece, a gorgeous snowman—eighteen inches tall and sporting a red-and-white scarf, a traditional pipe and stovepipe hat, soft brown eyes, and a joyful grin.

The snowman—we'd been calling him "Warner" around the office—was constructed completely of chocolate, of course. His body was white chocolate, his eyes were milk chocolate, and his hat and pipe were dark chocolate. The red scarf and his happy grin were of white chocolate tinted red. His body had been dusted with sugar so that it glittered like snow. He was displayed among drifts of puffy cotton.

Warner was a work of art, and Aunt Nettie had spent hours and hours building him, hidden in the back room so that he would come as a complete surprise at the opening.

Aunt Nettie flushed and beamed as she acknowledged the applause. When it stopped, she said, "I will ask a favor of next year's WinterFest committee, however. Could you pick a Yule log as your symbol? Or something else that's brown? Purists are sure to complain because I used white chocolate for this snowman—but a milk or dark chocolate snowman just didn't seem right."

Everyone chuckled, but unless they were chocolate snobs, they might not have grasped the full significance of her comment. Those purists she referred to claim that white chocolate isn't really chocolate at all, since it contains only cacao butter, but no cacao solids. I tend to agree with them. If I'm really hungry for something sweet, white chocolate is sugary enough to suit—I'll eat chocolate in any form—but it doesn't compare in flavor to dark chocolate with a high cacao content of seventy or eighty percent.

I thought about the smaller snowmen Aunt Nettie and

Dolly Jolly and her staff of chocolate experts—the ones I call the "hairnet ladies"—were making for the WinterFest promotion. These wouldn't be on sale until the festival officially opened the next day. The day before I'd grabbed up a box of a dozen—four of each color—to give to Fletcher Mendenhall. I wondered idly if the Lake Knapp police were eating them, or if they would languish in some evidence room until they were ruined.

I agreed with three people who made admiring remarks about Aunt Nettie's creation, then grabbed a glass of white wine and went into the art show. It was already crowded, and people were still pouring in.

I was immediately collared by Sarajane Harding, who was not only a member of the WinterFest committee, but a good friend of Aunt Nettie's.

"Lee, thanks for leaving the message to say Mendenhall wouldn't be coming Tuesday."

"I hated to leave you with an empty room."

"No problem. It turned out that I needed to make an emergency trip to Wal-Mart late that afternoon. Since Mendenhall didn't show up, I didn't have to give him dinner." Her dimples flashed. "You didn't dump that awful Mendenhall because you were trying to protect me, did you?"

"No, Sarajane. I dumped him because I didn't want to drive for an hour over icy roads with an amorous drunk. But I wouldn't have dumped him on you either, once I realized the state he was in."

"I assure you that after twenty years in the B and B biz, I know how to handle a drunk."

"I'm sure you do. But aren't you there alone at the inn this time of year?"

Sarajane spoke sharply. "Why do you ask?"

"I was just wondering how you would handle an inebriated guest."

"Oh. Well. Actually I have a friend staying with me right at the moment."

"How nice. Is she here tonight?"

"No! No, she decided to have an early evening. But, anyway, I'm not exactly alone at the inn right now."

"But how do you handle it when you are alone?"

"I wouldn't say there's a problem twice a year, Lee. Of course, I ask all the guests for references, plus credit card information or cash."

"But that's financial, isn't it? I mean, to make sure they'll pay the bill." Sarajane's bills are steep. "A good financial reputation won't stop obnoxious personal behavior."

"I have a lock on the door of my apartment, of course." Sarajane leaned close and smiled her sweet smile. "And I sleep with a pistol in the bedside table."

Sarajane slept with a pistol beside her? I was surprised, but I tried to joke her comment off. "If I need to come by your house late at night, I'll be sure to call first."

"Good idea. I find time for regular target practice. It's a habit I got into after my marriage broke up. I'm sure Nettie has told you my ex is in jail." She nodded firmly. Then she walked over to talk to Mayor Mike Herrera.

I stared after her. Sarajane's ex-husband was in jail? And she kept a pistol beside her bed? If Sarajane were threatened, would she actually use that weapon?

Somehow I didn't doubt that she would. Sarajane might look like a sweet little old lady, but those dimples were on the cheeks of a very hard head.

Had Aunt Nettie told me something about Sarajane's ex-husband being abusive? I'd have to ask. But I sure wouldn't approach Sarajane's inn without warning her I was coming. Joe, the former defense attorney, had assured me that the most unlikely people can resort to violence, and I had no reason not to believe him.

Except maybe I wouldn't believe Mary Samson could become violent. That thought of Mary becoming violent was a little too unlikely.

Mary was walking toward me, still looking worried. "Lee, is Joe right? Do I really need to tell the police about that phone call?"

"Joe spent five years as a defense attorney. He's had a lot of experience with investigation of crimes."

Mary looked as if she'd like to wring her hands, but she was holding a tall glass of something I assumed was ginger ale. "But the things that man on the phone said . . . the language he used . . . it's just too embarrassing to repeat."

"I assure you that the police will have heard much worse language."

"I suppose so. But he actually accused me . . . Well, Lee, could I tell you about it?"

"Of course, Mary. But is this a good time?"

"Oh, no! You're right. I could call you later."

"We're not planning to be out late. I'll call you when I get home."

Amos Hart, who had been standing behind Mary in the crowded room, picked that moment to put his hand on her shoulder, and Mary yelped as if he'd kicked her. She turned around, looking panicky.

"Oh, Mr. Hart! You startled me."

"I'm sorry, Mary. I just wanted to say you look very pretty tonight."

I was surprised by Amos' comment. Mary could have been pretty, but she wasn't wearing makeup, her hair was badly cut, and her fluffy dress was much too childish for a woman in her early to middle twenties. I would have loved to turn Mary over to a good stylist for a complete redo.

Maybe a complete redo would give her some confidence. Amos' innocuous comment on her appearance seemed to have thrown her into an emotional crisis. She blushed, stammered, and spilled her drink down the front of her dress. Then she turned and fled.

Amos looked appalled. "Was I that crude? I was just trying to be nice to that poor child."

"You were fine, Amos. Nobody ever told Mary that when you get a compliment all you have to do is say thanks."

"I had a compliment for your aunt, too. The big snowman is wonderful!"

"I'll tell her you said so. He'll be displayed in our window for the rest of the WinterFest."

"And the small snowmen are great, too! I really like the singing one: The way his mouth makes an 'O' is super."

"Yes, he's delightful. But where did you see him?"

"Weren't there some on the refreshment table?"

"I don't think so. They're not on sale until tomorrow."

Amos looked confused. "Then I don't know where it was."

I sipped my wine and decided it would be tactful to change the subject. "I'm looking forward to the choral concert next weekend. Are you pleased with the way it's going?"

"I'm hopeful. It's surprising how many good voices there are in a small town like Warner Pier. I think it's a tribute to the quality of choral music instruction in the schools and the churches."

"The churches? I thought most of our churches were too small to have real choir directors—except for your church, of course. Most churches here don't even have regular choirs."

"They don't in winter perhaps. Like everything in Warner Pier, the churches get larger when the summer people come, and the choirs follow that trend." I'd brought up a subject Amos had obviously studied, because he began to enumerate which of the Warner Pier churches had professional choir directors and which of them had active choirs. And how large those choirs were. I was amazed at the amount of information he had collected.

Amos was still lecturing me about the local choirs when Mozelle joined us. To my surprise, she touched Amos on the arm. "I don't feel compelled to stay all evening," she said. "We can leave whenever you've seen enough."

"We?" Since when were Amos and Mozelle "we"?

I nearly choked on my white wine. Instead I sipped it gently and tried not to show my surprise. "I haven't looked at a thing," I said. "I'd better start oozing—I mean, ogling! I'd better start ogling the art."

"That's exactly the right word for some of it," Amos said. "Ogle, I mean. I'm no art expert, but the meanings of some of the pieces are unmistakable, and not what I'd call uplifting."

I chuckled and tried to make the sound casual. "I'll look for the works with the most people around them. Controversy always brings crowds."

"They may not be controversial in Warner Pier," Mozelle said. "The town has grown more and more liberal artistically."

"I'm sorry to say I think you're right," Amos said. "Lee, that's why I believe you'd enjoy our church—even if you don't want to sing in my choir."

"I'm sorry, Amos. You lost me. What do you mean?"

He spoke earnestly. "I mean that you're from Texas. That's part of the Bible Belt. You probably grew up in conservative churches."

"Actually, in Prairie Creek the First United Methodist was considered scandalously liberal," I said. "I see Joe over there, and I need to tell him something. Bye."

I walked away, hoping that steam wasn't shooting out my ears. I hate it when people assume that because I'm from Texas I think a certain way. Texans tend to be independent thinkers, after all. It's not that I was insulted by being considered a religious conservative. I probably am conservative by some people's standards. It's that I hate being judged by where I grew up, especially by people who have never been in Texas and don't know one thing about the state. So there.

I'd calmed down by the time I'd made my way through the crowd and had reached Joe. I took his arm, just the way Mozelle had taken Amos'. "Seen anything you want to buy?"

"I thought the budget wouldn't allow art purchases?"

"Probably not. I haven't really looked at the show yet. Have you?"

"No. But I've seen all the people I needed to talk to."

We laughed and began to walk around and look at the art. The first-place winner, I decided, was the one Amos Hart had found offensive. It was an oil by an artist I didn't know and, yes, you didn't have to understand symbolism to get what it was about. I admired the colors and textures, but I was not tempted to put it in our living room.

Johnny Owens' reindeer had received an honorable mention. It was displayed in front of Mozelle's watercolor—her usual pale pastel beach scene. The first judge had obviously seen something in her work that I didn't or she wouldn't even be in the show.

I caught my breath when I saw the best of show. It was a dramatic photograph of a storm over Lake Michigan and had been taken by Ramona's husband, Bob Van Winkle-Snow. Bob himself, a blocky guy whose shoulder-length gray hair flew in all directions, was holding court in front of the photo.

"Oh, Bob!" I said. "It's stunning!"

Bob smiled. "I'm highly gratified that Dr. Harrison liked it. Believe me, if that jerk Mendenhall had judged the show it wouldn't have won a thing."

Chapter 8

I must have looked surprised, because Bob got defensive.

"Sorry if you don't think I should speak ill of the dead," he said.

"Neither of us will argue with your opinion of Mendenhall, no matter how bad it is," Joe said, "and I don't think the fact that he's dead changed any of his personal characteristics. I guess you knew the guy."

"We exchanged a few words. In fact, we exchanged them publicly. He was one of these dinosaurs who think photography isn't an art form."

I pointed to the photograph with the big rosette on the corner. "That's definitely art to me, Bob. It's beautiful to look at and moving emotionally. Where was it shot?"

Bob looked proud and began to tell where he had taken it and to describe the darkroom techniques he had used to heighten the storm clouds. No, he said, it wasn't computer enhanced.

"Though I do use the computer sometimes. That's one of the things idiots like Mendenhall won't accept."

The conversational group shifted then, and Joe and I moved on. But I moved on convinced that Bob VanWinkle-Snow was the person Mozelle had been talking about when she said Mendenhall had a public fight with a Warner Pier artist. Bob was the person she'd wanted to set up as a suspect without going to the police herself.

It was simply too coincidental that the dirt Mozelle was spreading around besmirched the husband of her archrival, Ramona. And Bob certainly wasn't making a secret of his feelings about Mendenhall. Didn't that indicate he wasn't concerned in his death?

As I walked away I was furious with Mozelle all over again. I became completely determined that I wouldn't mention what she had said to anybody. Not even to Sergeant Mc-Cullough. Not even if he asked.

Joe spoke in to my ear, which was the best way to communicate in the noisy room. "Hogan and Nettie asked us to go to dinner with them," he said. "I hope that's all right with you. You said you wanted to go home early."

"No, it's a good idea. I want to talk to Hogan."

As Aunt Nettie had said, what's the point of having a police chief in the family if you don't *use* him. I was dying to go over the whole Mendenhall situation with Hogan.

I began rehearsing my story as I hit the party's food table, determined to stick to veggies and not ruin my appetite for dinner. And there I came face-to-face with a fellow Winter-Fest committee member, Jason Foster, manager of the Warner Pier Conference Center and operator of its restaurant.

Since Jason was in charge of the reception, I wasn't surprised to see him standing behind the steamboat round. His long white chef's jacket, neckerchief, and George Washington–style queue made him look like an eighteenth-century dandy who had laid his velvet coat aside.

"Hi," I said. "I suppose you're too busy feeding the rest of us to get anything to eat yourself."

Jason grinned. "I sampled everything in the kitchen. How about some roast beef?" He deftly sliced a thin sliver of pink meat, and I caught it on a tiny piece of rye bread.

"I left the meeting early," Jason said, "so I didn't get to hear all you and Joe had to report on the big murder investigation."

"We didn't have anything startling to say—the Lake Knapp police are not confiding in us. The main thing, I guess, is that after I dumped Mendenhall at the motel, he may have tried to call someone in Warner Pier. I don't suppose he phoned you?"

"If he did, I didn't get the call." Jason leaned close to me. "To tell the truth, George finished hanging the show about seven, and I went home and had a stiff scotch. DeWitt's here, you know."

"No, I didn't know."

DeWitt was the grown son of Jason's partner, Casey. "He doesn't come often, does he?"

"No, but this year he's determined to spoil my Christmas by making me be polite when I'm home as well as when I'm at work." Jason grimaced. "Maybe I'm jealous. Anyway, I went to bed early and left DeWitt and Casey to their reminiscences. For one thing, I knew it was the last time I'd get any sleep for a couple of weeks."

"I think everyone was trying to gather strength for the big event," I said. "We're all afraid we'll have to work too hard—and afraid we won't."

Jason and I shared a smile. If the Winter Festival promotion went over well, Warner Pier merchants would be exhausted. If it flopped, they'd be standing around with nothing to do. In the one case, we'd all be tired, but happy. In the other we'd be less tired, but extremely unhappy. So we were hoping for exhaustion.

A half hour later lots of the art patrons were moving into the restaurant dining room for dinner, so Hogan and Joe suggested the four of us avoid the crowd by going to Herrera's. Aunt Nettie and I readily agreed.

"Maybe Aunt Nettie can get some peace there," I said. "She's the belle of the art show because of the success of her big snowman." Aunt Nettie smiled modestly.

Herrera's is one of four restaurants owned by Mike Herrera, a person who affects our lives in lots of ways. First, since he's the mayor of Warner Pier, he's Joe's boss in his one-day-a-week job as city attorney. Second, Mike is the father-in-law of one of my best friends, Lindy Herrera. Third, he dates Joe's mom. Fourth, he's a fellow businessman in our community.

This combination of connections proves one thing: Warner Pier is definitely a small town. As the old joke says, our town is too little to have a village idiot; we all have to take turns.

But Mike is no idiot. He's an intelligent and practical businessman. He's also the first Hispanic to hold an elective office in Warner Pier. I like and respect him. And his restaurants have great food.

Lindy was on duty at Herrera's that night, seating guests and acting as manager—probably because Mike had to be at the WinterFest reception in his civic capacity. Her primary job is to manage Mike's catering operation.

When the four of us said we wanted to talk, Lindy gave us a table in the corner. Herrera's is a class operation. Even during the summer rush it's quiet, and it was ultraquiet that night, less than two weeks before Christmas. The background music actually stayed in the background.

The restaurant was wearing its winter decor. Herrera's is right down on the river, and in the summer the French doors are left open, and diners can have tables on the deck. In the winter the French doors are covered with shutters and are flanked by burgundy velvet draperies. Paintings in dark tones replace the pale beach scenes Mike's hangs in summer.

I love all Mike's restaurants because he's a Texas native like me, and at his places I can get iced tea all year-round. But

Herrera's is the restaurant that makes me feel sophisticated and pampered.

Joe, Hogan, Aunt Nettie, and I all claimed that we had only lightly grazed the hors d'oeuvres table at the reception, so we ordered dinner, and Hogan made a little ritual out of choosing a bottle of wine for the table. Then Joe and I reported on Mendenhall's death and the day we'd had dealing with its effects.

Joe concluded with his deduction about Mendenhall's cell phone being missing.

Hogan nodded. "Sounds as if you're right, not that it means anything."

I was surprised at his reaction. "It doesn't mean anything? But won't the Lake Knapp cops want to find out who took it?"

"Sure. It's evidence—just like anything that's missing from the room. But they can trace his calls without having the phone. And whom do you think he called?"

"George had given him a list of the WinterFest committee. I'd expect him to call one of them. Anyway, at the meeting before the reception, Joe and I urged anyone who heard from Mendenhall to contact this Sergeant McCullough."

"Did anyone say they had talked to Mendenhall?"

"Not really. Mary Samson said she got a crank call from someone who sounded drunk. A lot of people said they hadn't been home last night. Most of them were out doing committee business—hanging the art show or at play rehearsal or something."

"So if Mendenhall tried to call them, he probably couldn't reach anyone." Hogan grinned. "What do you think he would have done next?"

I shrugged. "Gone out to eat? How would I know?"

Joe laughed. "I think I see what Hogan is getting at, Lee. And he's probably right."

"Right about what?"

"Mendenhall. Picture the guy. You had raised his hopes for an exciting evening, then dumped him in a cheap motel. He couldn't reach anybody who was interested in coming to rescue him. So what would he want next?"

"I don't know what you're getting at, Joe."

Aunt Nettie reached across the table and patted my hand. "Companionship, Lee."

"But . . ." I finally caught on. "Oh. You mean paid companionship. With a sleazy desk clerk like that motel had, he wouldn't have had any trouble finding it. I'm sure that guy has a list of numbers to call."

I'd left my run-in with the desk clerk out of the story earlier, so I recapped it, ending with Joe's crack about being late to Bible study.

Hogan laughed. "I wouldn't worry about that guy, Lee. I don't even think you need to worry about McCullough."

"He certainly seemed to consider both Joe and me suspects."

"McCullough may have wanted to give you that impression, but I have a feeling he was psyching you out. By now he will have called around—as a matter of fact this Detective Robertson called my office and left a message asking me to call him back tomorrow. McCullough will call the county attorney, or Mike Herrera, or other people down here. By tomorrow he'll know both you and Joe are considered solid citizens."

"But, Hogan, that won't let us off the hook if he thinks either of us really did something to Mendenhall."

"You're right. But the very fact that you're both on the WinterFest Committee means you're not the kind of people to bash a guy's head in and go off and leave him."

"How does being on the committee prove that?"

"Lee, I've investigated a lot of killings in motels. They all involved drugs, booze, prostitution, or wild parties of some kind. When you find a guy dead in a motel, you don't automatically think he's the victim of some complicated plot involving people he hardly knows from a strange town. You think he checked in there to participate in activities he couldn't participate in at home—and those activities tend to involve criminals of some kind. Prostitutes, drug dealers—stuff like that."

"That makes sense."

"McCullough will be wringing information out of that desk clerk, and I expect that by now he's got a lead on any 'companion' Mendenhall called. In fact, if he's any kind of a detective at all, he already knows which girls work those motels regularly."

Joe frowned. "Then you think Mendenhall got caught in some kind of badger game?"

"It's sounds possible, Joe. If I was in charge of the case, that's the line I'd follow first."

Hogan's comments eased my mind quite a bit. Maybe Joe and I weren't the top suspects in the death of Mendenhall. The knot in my stomach relaxed, and the conversation turned back to the art show and the people who had been there. I asked Aunt Nettie about Sarajane's husband; was he really in jail?

"I hope he's still there," she said. "He was awful. Nearly killed Sarajane the last time he beat her up."

"I can't picture a person as hardheaded as Sarajane in an abusive relationship."

"She didn't start out hardheaded, Lee. She had to become that way to survive. I admire her, particularly because her troubles made her care about other abused women."

Aunt Nettie stopped talking and gave a sidelong glance at Hogan. He smiled and looked at the ceiling.

"Sarajane used to be a very active supporter of the Holland women's shelter," Aunt Nettie said firmly. "Hogan, please pass the butter."

When my dinner came I enjoyed my chicken in lemon sauce, my green salad, and my hard rolls. I ordered coffee instead of dessert, but I did take a bite of Joe's cheesecake.

By the time I finished the second cup of coffee, I could think about Mendenhall's death without feeling panicky. I told Hogan so.

"You've taken a big load off my mind, Hogan. After talking to you, I do not see how McCullough can be anything more than an annoyance to either Joe or me."

Hogan nodded. "He may have some more questions, Lee, but unless he finds something else to link you to Mendenhall, I fail to see how he can give you any more trouble."

"You've also relieved my mind about something else," I said. "I knew neither Joe nor I killed Mendenhall. But because of the missing cell phone, I was afraid he called somebody on the committee, and that person went into Lake Knapp and killed him. Lots of people wouldn't know that taking the cell phone wouldn't mean the police couldn't trace Mendenhall's calls anyway. So I was regarding my fellow committee members with suspicion. Now I see that that's not likely either."

I wrapped my paisley shawl around me and clutched my tiny purse as we got up to walk toward the entrance, where Herrera's provided a cloakroom. It was nearly nine thirty, so Lindy had abandoned her greeting spot near the front door. She evidently saw us leaving, because she appeared from somewhere behind the scenes and spoke.

"Is one of you the person with 'The Hallelujah Chorus' on your cell phone?"

Joe and I both whipped our heads in her direction. "What do you mean?" I said.

"Someone's left their phone in the cloakroom, and it's

been belting out 'The Hallelujah Chorus' off and on for the past half hour."

And, precisely on cue, a tinny electronic version of Handel's seasonal hit began to peel out. Joe and I nearly knocked each other flat getting through the door of the cloakroom.

Then I heard Hogan. "Don't touch it," he said.

Joe and I walked along the hanging coats, listening carefully. It was Joe who reached out and plucked a full-length camel hair coat off its hook.

"The Hallelujah Chorus" was coming from its left-hand pocket.

I gasped. Then I yelled. "That's my coat!"

"Don't take the phone out," Hogan said. "Let me preserve it some way."

Joe carried the coat out and draped it over a nearby table. Then Hogan gently turned the pocket inside out. A standard cell phone—a popular brand in a popular color—fell onto the table.

"Oh, dear, Hogan," Aunt Nettie said, "you had made Lee feel so much better, and now this."

My stomach had tied itself into another knot, and I readily grasped what Aunt Nettie was talking about.

Hogan had said Joe and I were probably not serious suspects in Mendenhall's killing, but he'd added one condition. "Unless McCullough finds something else to link you to Mendenhall," Hogan had said.

And now Mendenhall's missing cell phone had been found in my coat pocket.

Chocolate Comes to the U.S.

The earliest chocolate manufacturer in what is today the United States is believed to have been an Irishman, John Hannon, who came to Dorchester, Massachusetts, in 1765. Although much information about Hannon remains unsubstantiated, a Boston history Web site says he apparently had learned how to make chocolate in London. In Dorchester Hannon got financial backing from a man named James Baker.

Hannon's fate is a mystery. He was reportedly lost at sea, but a tale that he merely ran away from a difficult wife also pops up. At any rate, he disappeared from Dorchester, leaving his company in the care of James Baker. Baker bought out Mrs. Hannon and thus was born Baker's Chocolate, a company that is still around. Today it's owned by Kraft Foods.

For a hundred years Baker's remained a "family" firm, although the links of family ownership stretched from father to son to son to brother-in-law to a step-nephew, Henry Pierce, who oversaw the incorporation of the company in 1895.

Chapter 9

Hogan, Aunt Nettie, Joe, and I all leaned over the cell phone, our heads almost touching.

I spoke softly. "Should we answer it?"

"Don't touch it," Hogan said. "There's not much chance, but we'll have to check for fingerprints. Who's the call from?"

"There's no name," Joe said.

I got a glimpse of the number on the tiny screen—I thought the number ended with three consecutive fours—before "The Hallelujah Chorus" stopped midmelody.

"Oh, dear," Aunt Nettie said, "now we can't tell who was calling."

"It's stored in the phone," Hogan said.

We all acted calm, but I wasn't feeling that way. I seriously considered falling down on the floor, screaming, kicking madly, and chewing on one of the restaurant's white linen tablecloths. A complete collapse seemed to be a proper reaction. I didn't want to deal with this.

How could that phone be in the pocket of my coat? It simply wasn't possible.

"I did not take Mendenhall's phone," I said.

Joe, Hogan, and Aunt Nettie ignored me, so I spoke again.

"I did not stick it in my pocket by accident. And if I had taken it on purpose, I'm smart enough to turn it off. And I wasn't even wearing that coat yesterday."

Aunt Nettie patted my hand. "Don't dither, Lee dear."

"But how the heck did that phone get in my pocket?"

When Aunt Nettie answered, she sounded a bit testy. "Someone put it there, obviously! We just need to figure out who and why."

Luckily, most of the tables in Herrera's were now empty. I threw myself down in a chair at one of them and stared at the ceiling, considering Aunt Nettie's question. Who had put that phone in my pocket? And why had he or she done it?

And for that matter, when?

That question was easy to answer, of course. I only wore my full-length camel hair coat when I dressed up. A fashion expert might think it a bit casual for evening, but it was a lot less casual than my ski jacket, and the camel hair and the ski jacket were the only two warm winter coats I owned. My wardrobe did not include a smooth flannel coat with a velvet collar, a satin opera cape lined in mink, or a chinchilla jacket.

I'd worn the ski jacket when I went to pick up Mendenhall, and I'd worn that jacket to the office the next morning—was that still today?—then on to Lake Knapp to be questioned by the police. The WinterFest reception was the first occasion I'd had to get out the camel hair coat since Mendenhall landed in Michigan.

I'd put the coat on at home—without checking the pockets for stray cell phones—and I wore it to Warner Point. I went into the WinterFest office for the committee meeting. I tossed my coat onto a table along the side of the room, along with all the other coats of the committee members. And I left it there when I went in to the reception. Joe had retrieved it when we left Warner Point two and a half hours later. Then I put the coat on again—no, I didn't feel in the pockets that time either—and wore it to Herrera's, where Joe hung it in the cloakroom for me.

I seriously doubted that someone had broken into our house and put the phone in the coat pocket. It was more likely that the culprit had put the phone in my pocket while the coat was in the meeting room at Warner Point or in the cloakroom at Herrera's. And the cloakroom at Herrera's wasn't a likely spot, because there were only a few people there. I knew several of them by sight, and Lindy would probably have credit card information on the rest of them, so that could be checked out easily.

No, the most likely place for the phone to have gotten into my pocket was the meeting room at Warner Point.

"Darn!" I said. "We're right back to the WinterFest committee. Somebody in that group of people put the phone in my pocket."

Hogan asked Lindy to bring a paper sack and some tongs from the kitchen, and he carefully put the phone in the sack. He said he would lock it in the police station vault overnight and call McCullough the next morning.

"I have one question," he said. "Lee, is there any way to identify this coat as yours?"

"As mine?"

"Yes. Nettie, Joe, and I—and probably Lindy—have all seen you wear this coat. If you asked me to go into a room full of coats and bring yours out, I could probably narrow the choice down to two or three coats. But could a person who doesn't know you well do that?"

As an answer, I flipped the coat open and showed him the lining. The initials "S," "L," and "M" were embroidered inside.

"Aunt Nettie gave me this coat the first Christmas after I moved to Warner Pier," I said. "It's a good coat, and she had it monogrammed. Of course, you'd have to know my full name, my maiden name. Susanna Lee McKinney."

"But since you've been married just six months, most people remember at least the L and the M," Aunt Nettie said.

Hogan grimaced. "That doesn't eliminate anybody, does it?"

He said I could wear the coat home, so I put it on, and Joe and I went to the van. After the surprise of finding the cell phone, it seemed anticlimactic simply to go home and get ready for bed.

But what else could we do?

By the time I had washed my face and put on my flannel nightgown, I'd thought of something.

When Joe came out in his pajamas, I was sitting at the dining room table with a yellow legal pad. "I'm making a list of the WinterFest committee," I said, "along with what they had to say about last night."

"Last night?"

"The time when Mendenhall would have been using his cell phone to call people. I want to know where they say they were."

Joe sat down and scratched his head. "Lee, the police will be looking into that. In fact, I'm sure they've already contacted Mendenhall's phone server and have a list of calls both to and from that cell phone."

"Yes, but I think they're mainly going to be interested in the calls he made to my cell phone."

"Your cell phone? Would Mendenhall have had your cell phone number?"

"Yes. I called Mendenhall from outside the airport. It would be stored in his 'recent calls' file. Plus I'm on that list of committee members."

Joe sighed. "So you still think he called someone on the committee, and they met him, killed him, and took his phone?"

"Who else could have put that phone in my pocket?"

"About half the people in Warner Pier, plus dozens more from all over southwest Michigan. A few from Chicago. Anybody who was at the reception could have done it."

I stared at Joe. "But my coat was in the room where the committee met, not out in the main check room for the reception."

"And the door to that room was open. Anybody could have walked in there, Lee. How many people were at the reception? Two hundred? Three hundred?"

I stared at my legal pad and thought about what Joe was saying.

"I know you're right." I sighed. "Anybody in west Michigan could have killed Mendenhall, and about two hundred fifty of them could have put the phone in my pocket. But figuring out the whereabouts of the WinterFest committee members makes me feel that I'm doing something—something more than just sitting here waiting for the Lake Knapp police to decide I'm the guilty party and arrest me."

Joe took my hand. "Or waiting for them to decide I'm the guilty party and arrest me. You're right. Let's make a list."

I picked up my file folder, the one with the WinterFest paperwork in it. "At least I have a list of the full committee. Starting with Ramona."

I wrote "Ramona VanWinkle-Snow" at the top of the page. "It seems to me that Ramona said she was at George's gallery, dealing with some sort of last-minute problem. And later she was at home."

"That would mean neither she nor George could have gone to Lake Knapp to kill Mendenhall."

"It depends on how late he died. She said they were through by seven."

"They're in the clear for half the evening."

"Yes, but we don't know anything about Bob."

"Ramona's husband? Where does he fit in?"

I told Joe about Mozelle's clumsy attempt to link "a local artist" to Mendenhall. "After what Bob said about Mendenhall, I'm convinced he was the one she was talking about. It may be far-fetched, but if Mendenhall called Ramona's house, Bob could have taken the call and decided to take care of Mendenhall permanently. But surely he wouldn't have later volunteered that information about their problems."

"Killing Mendenhall doesn't sound like something either Ramona or Bob would do."

"For the moment, we've got to forget that these are people we know, Joe, and just look at their opportunities to commit the crime."

I looked the list of committee members over. "That takes care of Ramona and George. Yes, either of them could have gone to Grand Rapids later in the evening and offed Mendenhall.

"Now Maggie said she was at dress rehearsal from six o'clock on."

"So she's not likely."

"Jason said he went home as soon as the show had been hung, ate dinner, and went straight to bed. But his partner, Casey, and Casey's son where there, so he's not too likely. He would have had to climb out a window and hitchhike to Lake Knapp. But I don't think anybody else said where they were."

"And the only one who admitted Mendenhall had called was Mary Samson."

"Mary!" I gasped. "Oh, my gosh! I told her I'd call as soon as I got home."

"It's a little late now," Joe said. "After ten thirty."

"She was worried, but I didn't understand just what her problem was. I'll call her first thing in the morning."

I flipped over to the second page of the list of committee members. "I'll put her number up by the phone on a sticky, so I won't forget."

I wrote down the Warner Pier prefix—there's only one, of course—then looked at the list. "One-four-four-four," I said.

Then my heart did a flip. I grabbed Joe's arm. "Oh, no!"

"What's the matter?"

"Joe, when Mendenhall's cell phone rang, did you get a look at the number that the call came from?"

"I may have, but it didn't make a big impression."

"I hate to sound like a real number person. . . ."

"You are a real number person, Lee. That's the reason you were able to get Nettie's business back in the black. And its the reason we're arguing over Christmas gifts and the way I handle my business Visa."

I ignored his comment. "I may be completely wrong. But the number that called the cell phone and unleashed 'The Hallelujah Chorus' had three fours. And Mary's number ends in one-four-four-four."

Joe and I stared at each other. Then he got up and brought the portable phone from the kitchen. "Call her," he said.

"It's really late."

"Call her."

I punched in Mary's number. The phone rang four times and was picked up by the answering machine.

I waited for the beep. "Mary, are you there? It's Lee."

Mary didn't answer the phone.

I frowned at the gadget in my hand. "I don't like that. Mary certainly seemed to be planning to go straight home from the reception."

"She might be in the shower," Joe said. "She might be in bed."

"I'll call again."

Once again I punched in Mary's number. Once again I got the answering machine. I hollered at it. "Mary! It's Lee! I need to talk to you!"

Once again Mary failed to pick the phone up.

Joe and I looked at each other. Then we spoke in unison. "Let's call Hogan."

I felt pretty confident that Hogan and Aunt Nettie wouldn't be in bed yet, since we'd all left Herrera's less than an hour earlier. Sure enough, Hogan answered on the second ring. I quickly outlined my suspicion that the call to Mendenhall's cell phone had come from Mary Samson's phone.

Hogan spoke firmly. "It won't hurt if we run a welfare check on her."

"Joe and I can go over there," I said. "If the patrol car pulls up in her drive, it might scare poor Mary to death."

"You don't need to get out again."

"I'd feel better if we did."

Joe was already pulling on his jeans. We were on our way to Mary's house within five minutes.

Hogan and Aunt Nettie met us at the bridge over the Warner River. Hogan blinked his lights, and they followed us. I had trouble finding the house. Like us, Mary lived in a semirural part of Warner Pier, though she was near the river, and we were near the lake. We missed her turn the first time, but finally our van and Aunt Nettie's blue Buick pulled up in the drive.

Mary's house—as I said, she had inherited it from her parents—was a small 1940s frame house with a steep roof. The front porch light wasn't on, but there was a light on the garage, where it would illuminate the path from the drive to the house.

Joe and I got a flashlight from the glove compartment, and we tramped through the snow to get to the front porch. We both stamped the snow off our feet on the porch, then I looked for a doorbell.

"I'd have thought Mary would have heard the cars and looked out to see who's here," I said. I pushed the doorbell button, and I could hear the bell peal inside the house.

But no one came to the door. No one seemed to be moving inside the house. I pushed the button again.

By that time Hogan was behind us. "I'll walk around and check the back," he said. He stepped off the porch, keeping his own flashlight trained on the snow.

I rang the doorbell. Then I knocked. Then I called out, "Mary! It's Lee and Joe! Let us in!"

Finally—finally—I heard movement inside. "Here she is! I guess we woke her up."

But when the door opened, the person who opened it wasn't Mary. It was Hogan.

"Hogan!" I said. "How did you get in?"

"Back door was standing open."

"Where's Mary?"

"Lee, you and Nettie go on home."

"Go home? Hogan, what's wrong?"

"I've already called for the EMTs, but . . ."

"What's happened to Mary?"

"She's on the kitchen floor, Lee. I'm sure she's dead."

Chapter 10

Joe, Aunt Nettie, and I sat in the van until the Warner Pier patrol car—the only one on duty—got there. Then we left.

Hogan had made it clear he didn't want us contaminating his crime scene, so we hadn't gone inside the house. But I felt bad about leaving Mary.

"If I'd talked to Mary at the party, maybe this wouldn't have happened," I said. I didn't have a Kleenex, so I snuffled loudly.

"That's silly, Lee," Aunt Nettie said. She handed me a tissue. "First, you don't know that Mary's death had anything to do with whatever she wanted to tell you. Second, if she had told you, it might not have made any difference. Third, if she'd made a real effort to talk to you, you would have listened."

"Mary was too shy to make a real effort," Joe said, "about anything that involved talking, at least."

I continued to feel bad. When we got to Aunt Nettie and Hogan's house, there was no discussion of our going home. Joe and I went in with her, and I got out the cups while Aunt Nettie made hot chocolate. The real kind, Mexican style, using solid chocolate melted slowly in milk, with stick cinnamon and two cloves added.

Yes, chocolate helps meet all crises. I drank two cups and felt much calmer by the time Hogan called.

Joe and I could go home, he said. Michigan State Police officials—they're responsible for helping small towns investigate serious crime—were on the way. Hogan would stay on the scene. He left out the words "probably all night," but we all knew that was what would happen.

Joe and I urged Aunt Nettie to come home with us, and finally she agreed to be an overnight guest in what had once been her own home. I wouldn't say any of us slept much, but at least we comforted one another.

At seven a.m. I had just turned on the coffeemaker when I saw headlights in our drive, and Hogan came to the kitchen door.

He looked exhausted, and he said only one word. "Coffee."

Joe, Aunt Nettie, and I took the hint, and none of us said anything until Hogan had had one cup of coffee, and the bacon, eggs, and English muffins were on the table.

Then Hogan spoke. "You two will have to make statements for VanDam."

Joe and I both nodded. Alex VanDam is a state police lieutenant who has been assigned to the area that includes Warner Pier for several years. Joe and I both knew him, and I sighed with relief. VanDam would be a lot easier to deal with than Sergeant McCullough of the Lake Knapp police.

That reminded me. "What about McCullough?"

"He'll still be involved, but VanDam may rein him in a little. We're working on the assumption that the two deaths are connected."

Hogan had worked all night and hadn't had the benefit of two cups of Aunt Nettie's hot chocolate to make the time go easier. I bit my tongue, putting off my questions until he'd had time to eat. After his second egg over easy and his third

English muffin and his fourth strip of bacon, he sighed deeply and refilled his coffee mug from the carafe on the table.

"I suppose you all want to know what happened," he said.

We spoke in unison. "Yes."

Hogan said that Mary's back door had been standing ajar, and he had found her body in the kitchen. Like Mendenhall, she'd been beaten to death.

"Was there a weapon?" Joe asked.

"Something flat and heavy. There was a lot of blood." Hogan shrugged. I knew he would hedge until the lab report came back.

He went on with his report. "Mary was wearing her coat and that dress she had on at the party. The bedroom window had been jimmied. Apparently somebody broke in and was waiting for her."

He took a drink of coffee. "But Mary had a lot of spunk. The kitchen was a mess. I think her attacker had to chase her all around the room. Chairs were turned over. Stuff had been swept off shelves."

I dried my eyes on my paper napkin. "I just can't believe this. Poor Mary! She was so meek and mild. How could anyone be heartless enough to kill her?"

At that point the phone rang. I answered. It was our neighbor, Charlie Bailey. "Did I see Hogan Jones over at your house?"

"Yes, he's here."

"Well, Annie Van Raalte called. She lives over by the Samson house. What happened over there?"

I knew it was the first of many calls. The Warner Pier grapevine was in full swing already.

Aunt Nettie and Hogan went home, and Joe and I let the answering machine pick up everything else. Neither of us had time to fool with a million phone calls. We needed to get ready for work. When they didn't get us at home, all those people would call my office or Joe's boat shop anyway.

When I headed for TenHuis Chocolade, I took along that list of WinterFest committee members—the one that listed their whereabouts at the time Mendenhall had been killed. Maybe I could make some phone calls of my own.

I decided the first person I had to talk to—even though I already knew where she said she'd been Thursday night—was Ramona. As soon as I was at my desk, I punched in the number of Snow Photography.

Ramona picked up the phone on the first ring. She spoke before I could identify myself. "Thanks for calling me back, Lee."

"Nice to know you have caller ID, Ramona." I made a mental note that Ramona must have been one of the people whose calls we had ignored that morning. "How are you?"

"I'm upset. What happened to Mary Samson?"

I gave her a sketchy version. Very sketchy. I left out the parts about Mendenhall's phone being found in my pocket and about the call on it coming from Mary's house—maybe— and about someone chasing Mary around the kitchen with something heavy and flat. I didn't even want to think about that part, and I was sure Hogan wouldn't want me to tell it.

Ramona didn't comment until I was through. Then she asked a question. "Why did you call Mary? I mean, it must have been late."

I'd already prepared an answer to that one. "Mary asked me to call. She said she wanted to discuss something with me, and I said I'd call her when I got home. Did you talk to her at the reception?"

"Only a few minutes."

"Did she say anything to you?"

"Nothing unusual. I told her I was delighted with the turnout for the reception, and that I thought she deserved most of the credit because of the great publicity campaign she ran. You can imagine how she reacted."

"Turned red and stammered. I don't suppose she said anything about a problem or question she had."

"What do you mean?"

"I'm looking for a clue to why she wanted me to call her."

"You won't get one from me. Mary was so pitifully shy. She communicated so well in writing, but face-to-face . . ."

"Yes, that was a different story." I took a deep breath. "I have a question for you, Ramona. What was going on on Wednesday night?"

"Wednesday night?"

"Night before last. You and George said you were hashing out some problem."

"Oh. That." Ramona was silent. "It was just something about one of the art show entries. It was the first time I'd seen them all."

"Oh. I thought you were at George's gallery."

"We were."

"But the show was hung at Warner Point."

Ramona sighed. "It wasn't a big deal, Lee. I went by Warner Point and looked at the show just after George had left. Jason let me in to see it. After I'd seen it, I had a question. So I tracked George down at the gallery and stopped to talk to him."

"How long were you there?"

"I don't really know." Ramona was losing her patience. "He was obviously trying to leave for some reason, kept looking at his watch, so I didn't stay long. Does it matter? George and I are not working by the hour."

Ramona had reminded me sternly about my place on the WinterFest committee. Finances. I was the bookkeeper, and that was all.

JoAnna Carl

"I guess it doesn't," I said. "I was just trying to figure out . . . I'm sure you were exhausted after the reception last night. Were you and Bob able to go straight home?"

"I did. Bob had some darkroom work to do down here. Listen, Lee, I see customers hovering outside our door. I'll talk to you later."

She hung up, leaving me wondering if I knew any more than I had before I called.

I pulled out my yellow legal pad and noted her answers on my list. She had been with George Jenkins at his gallery early on the night Mendenhall died. Later she'd been home alone with her husband. On Thursday night, when Mary was killed, Ramona had been at home, and Bob had being doing some work at the shop.

Next I called George Jenkins.

George also had to hear all I knew about Mary's death. But when I quizzed him on the problem he and Ramona had been hashing out, he laughed. "Ramona was having an attack of overconscientiousness."

"What about?"

"About Bob's entry in the art show. She hadn't known that he entered until she peeked at the show after it had been hung."

"Do you mean the storm photograph that won best of show? I loved it."

"Yes, it's great. In fact, both Ramona and I know enough about art to see that it was one of the best entries. Or most judges would place it near the top. Ramona was afraid that if it won, the sharper tongues of the local art scene would say it was nepotism."

"But at that time you all thought Mendenhall was going to be judging the show. Bob told Joe and me that Mendenhall hated photography and wouldn't have given it the prize."

George gave a small whistle. "Ramona didn't say anything

about that, and I hadn't heard it. Maybe she was really afraid that Bob's work would be ignored. Anyway, we had a discussion about his entry, and I finally brought her around. I don't think she relished the idea of telling Bob the photograph ought to be withdrawn, so she gave in."

"How late did this discussion last?"

"Oh, until seven o'clock or so. Why?"

"Just wondering who would have been available to talk to Mendenhall. If he called them."

"He called the gallery earlier—probably just after you dropped him off at the motel. The message he left was close to incoherent. But he didn't call back on that phone, and when he called my cell, he didn't make sense."

"Where were you later?"

George paused. "Oh, I had to go to Wal-Mart. Lee, I have to get busy. I'll talk to you later." George hung up.

That was the second brush-off I'd gotten. I made more notes on my yellow pad. By then it was a half hour after the time I should have been working, so I put the list aside and began to check my e-mail, printing out orders that had come in that way. Dolly Jolly, Aunt Nettie's chief assistant, brought me a list of supplies she needed delivered.

We set up a display of the small snowman, and I told Aunt Nettie that Amos Hart had said he admired them. "Did you give him an advance peek?"

"No. He was just being polite, Lee. He's that way. Always tries to give everyone a compliment."

The UPS man came, bringing some Christmas gift boxes Aunt Nettie seemed very glad to see. Tourists were wandering in, and the two teenage counter girls were selling boxes of snowmen, along with the occasional double-fudge bonbon ("layers of milk and dark chocolate fudge with a dark chocolate coating") or Midori coconut truffle ("very creamy all-white chocolate truffle, flavored with melon and rolled in coconut"). The coconut truffles look like tiny snowballs, and they get very popular around the holidays.

Mary Samson might be dead, but the regular routine was going on at TenHuis Chocolade, just the way it probably was all over Warner Pier. Regular routine is soothing to all of us, and the churning in my stomach slowed down.

Until Sergeant McCullough of the Lake Knapp police came in.

I hadn't glanced up when the outside door opened, so I didn't know McCullough was there until he was filling up the door to my office, blocking my exit, and making me feel trapped.

His white hair and mustache were just as beautiful as ever, and his smile was just as broad. "Hell-o, Mrs. Woodyard."

I fought down panic. "Hello, Sergeant McCullough. Please have a sit. I mean, a seat!" I bit my tongue, but it was too late. I'd twisted my tongue and revealed my nervousness. I spoke again. "I'm waiting for Lieutenant VanDam to call me to make a statement."

"I am not waiting for you to make a statement. I am going to make one myself. Right now." McCullough smiled more broadly than ever, but now his smile was not friendly. It was aggressive, mean. He was doing his best to scare me. And he was succeeding.

I sat completely still. Maybe I was too scared to move, but I like to think that my beauty pageant training kicked in. Keep quiet. Don't say anything if you're not sure what to say. Look poised, even if you don't feel that way. So I simply sat there and looked at him.

"Oh, you've got the cops down here buffaloed," Mc-Cullough said. He was still smiling, and his voice was low. "Little Miss Texas beauty, batting your eyelashes and looking innocent. You fall over two bodies in two days. Two of 'em! You admit you were the last person to see one victim and among the last to see the other! But I mustn't haul you in. Oh, no! A few questions might damage your looks!"

He leaned across the desk. "Don't count on it, babe! You can't get by on looks forever. I can throw you to the wolves anytime I want to."

Then he stood up, still smiling. "And here's the state police detective to ask you a few questions."

I guess I'd been hypnotized. Alex VanDam had walked right up to my office, and I hadn't seen him coming.

McCullough had kept his voice low. I realized that Alex VanDam hadn't heard what the Lake Knapp detective had said.

My head was spinning, and my heart was pounding. What should I do? Scream? Yell at McCullough? Burst into tears?

My office was so small I had room for only one visitor's chair. McCullough had to get up and go out into the shop to allow VanDam room to get in. While they were changing places, I decided what to do.

I greeted VanDam and motioned him into the chair. Then I stepped to the door, craning my head around McCullough. I waved at the girl behind the counter.

"Please bring a half dozen chocolates in for my guests," I said. "An assortment."

I motioned to McCullough. "Sergeant, behind you, there in the shop, is an extra chair. If you want to talk to me, please feel free to bring it in and sit down."

I went back to my chair, and I sat on my hands so that neither McCullough nor VanDam could see that they were shaking.

I turned to VanDam, deliberately ignoring McCullough. "Nice of you to come by. I thought you'd be summoning me to your headquarters."

"We will. This is just preliminary. Informal. Hogan says Mary Samson asked you to call her last night. Do you know why?"

"No, Lieutenant, I have no idea, and I've been kicking myself all day because I didn't just take her aside someplace and demand to know what she wanted to talk about."

"So you have no idea?"

I sighed. "At the WinterFest committee meeting, Joe and I had urged everyone to tell the Lake Knapp police if Dr. Mendenhall called them. Nobody there popped up and said he had, except Mary. She said she'd had a crank call from someone who sounded drunk. She seemed really disturbed when Joe and I said it might have been Mendenhall."

"Had he said something that frightened her?"

"Anything frightened Mary. But she seemed most afraid that she would have to repeat what he had said. It must have been obscene. Or at least it seemed obscene to Mary."

VanDam nodded, then asked me about my movements during the previous evening. When I said Joe and I had gone directly from the reception to Herrera's to have dinner with Hogan and Aunt Nettie, McCullough growled deep in his throat, and VanDam gave him a look. I'm not sure how to characterize that look—stern, maybe, or meaningful—but McCullough didn't say anything more. I concluded that he was unhappy because I had an alibi of sorts. Of course, we didn't know for sure when Mary had been killed. It was possible the phone call to Mendenhall's cell phone was made before she died.

"What time did you get home?" VanDam asked.

"It was around ten," I said.

"And you didn't go out again?"

"Not until I got worried about Mary—because I thought the call to Mendenhall's phone might have come from her house."

VanDam glanced at McCullough again. "Actually," he said, "I might as well tell you this. A couple named McNutt—"

"Sure. Maggie and Ken."

"They invited Ms. Samson to have dinner with them, there at the Warner Point restaurant. So she left for home around nine. We assume she got home about nine fifteen."

"Oh." I swallowed hard. At least Mary hadn't been alone on her last evening. I reached into my top drawer and pulled out a Kleenex. "Sorry," I said.

"But that leaves you and Joe on your own at the time Mary was killed." VanDam was completely deadpan, but McCullough smirked. I realized that the Lake Knapp detective must be pushing VanDam to use this line of questioning.

The realization made me mad. "Yes, Joe and I were together all evening," I said. "We could have combined our efforts and killed Mary. Do you want to take casts of our shoes? Examine our clothes for bloodstains?"

VanDam glared. "I'll settle for a look in your car, Lee. It's just routine."

"I realize that, Lieutenant VanDam." I reached in my desk drawer, took my keys out of the side pocket of my purse, and shoved them across the desk to him. "Here. The van is sitting in the alley. White. Dallas Cowboys sticker on the back window."

"Do you want to come?"

"No, thank you. I have work to do."

I led VanDam and McCullough back through the workroom and the break room, then opened the back door for them. I let the heavy metal door slam behind them, and I went back to my desk.

I had almost stopped seething ten minutes later, when VanDam came back.

"You'd better come out here, Lee," he said.

"I trust you and the sergeant to look the situation over."

"Don't be snotty, Lee. We need to ask you something."

Mystified, I followed him through the workroom and the

break room and out the back door. The rear of my van was popped open, and McCullough was standing under the hatch.

"What is it?" I said.

Silently, VanDam pointed. "Do you have an explanation for this?"

I followed his gesture and saw that he was pointing to an old-fashioned iron skillet.

It was lying on floor of the van. And it was surrounded by reddish brown stains.

It didn't take a genius to figure out that the iron skillet had probably come from Mary Samson's kitchen and had been used to beat her to death.

Chapter 11

If I'd felt like chewing a tablecloth when Mendenhall's cell phone was found in my pocket, that feeling was complete calm compared to the way I felt when I saw that skillet. It might as well have had "murder weapon" painted on it in luminous paint.

Aunt Nettie came out into the alley to see what was going on, and later she told me I was as pale as her big white-chocolate snowman. But I didn't get hysterical or break into sobs.

"Lieutenant VanDam, I've never seen that skillet before in my life," I said.

"Hmmm," he answered.

VanDam said the skillet would have to be tested. A technician appeared, bagged the skillet, marked it as evidence, then cut the stain out of the carpet that covered the floor of the van. He bagged that, too.

McCullough smiled like a proud grandpa through the whole procedure. I bit my tongue to keep from telling him that if I ever murdered anybody, it wouldn't be a harmless person like Mary Samson. It would be him. And it would be justifiable homicide.

They didn't arrest me.

After watching for a few minutes, I turned and walked

back into the break room and sat down on the comfortable couch Aunt Nettie provides for employees. It was Aunt Nettie who went to the phone and called Joe. Unfortunately, he wasn't at his shop, and he wasn't answering his cell phone. She left messages both places.

Then Aunt Nettie sat down beside me. "Listen, Lee," she said, "you go home or go out to hunt Joe down or do whatever you need to do. Don't worry about the shop today." She gave me a hug.

I shook my head. "Joe will call when he can. There's no point in chasing around town after him. It seems anticlimactic, but I guess I'll go back to work."

"If you need a lawyer . . ."

"Last night you said there's no point in having a police chief in the family if you don't use him. The same thing goes for having a lawyer in the family, I guess. I may need legal help, but I don't want to move on that without talking to Joe first."

Then I stood up and went through the workroom to my office. I wouldn't say I worked very effectively, but I did work. In fact, I had a panicky feeling that I'd better get as much done as I could before they arrested me.

I didn't quite abandon my efforts to call all the Winter-Fest committee members and check their alibis. I caught Johnny Owens at his studio.

He obviously had people there, apparently WinterFest tourists he hoped might buy something. So I asked him to call me back. In a half hour, he did.

"Hey, hey!" he said. "Made a sale."

"Congratulations! At your prices, one sale means a successful weekend."

"Well, I agreed to come down on price a little. Why did you call?"

I had decided simply to be blunt. "Johnny, I'm asking all

of the members of the WinterFest committee what they were doing Tuesday night."

There was a moment of silence. "I don't think I'll tell you. It's too embarrassing."

"Aw, come on, Johnny. Joe and I really need to find that out."

"You're getting into my secret vices, Lee."

I was afraid to ask. So I didn't say anything.

Johnny chuckled. "Oh, well, it'll ruin my tough-guy image, but I'll tell you. I was watching a DVD of *Ratatouille*."

For a second the word meant nothing to me. Rat-a-tat? Something about a drum? Then I remembered. "The movie? The cartoon about the rat who wants to be a chef?"

"Right. You've caught me in my secret vice. Animated films. I have a huge collection."

"I wouldn't call that a vice, Johnny."

"It's kind of a crazy thing for a grown man to do. But I've always loved cartoons. My childhood ambition was to be an animator. That's what got me interested in art."

I thought of Johnny's giant metal pieces, created with a welding torch and sledgehammer. "You certainly got away from your original interest." Then I remembered the tiny delicate drawings that Johnny made when he doodled. "Except for those little people you draw when you're bored. And our snowman mascot."

Johnny laughed. "Maybe I'll turn to cartooning yet. It ought to pay more than weird metal sculptures. But the cops already asked me about this, Lee. Apparently Mendenhall did try to call me. My number was in his phone records, but I didn't talk to him."

"Had you turned the phone off?"

"No. My Chicago dealer phoned about seven thirty, and we talked for forty-five minutes. Mendenhall must have called while the phone was tied up."

We said good-bye, promising to wave at each other at the opening of the play that evening. I hung up, frustrated. So far the only person who had a real alibi for Tuesday, when Mendenhall was killed, was Maggie McNutt, who had been at play rehearsal all evening. And Maggie would never kill anybody while a play was in production; she would be so concentrated on her rehearsals that she wouldn't notice anybody needed killing.

I hadn't checked on Mozelle or Amos Hart—I was still surprised that they had been together for the art show opening—and I resolved to do that. I was reaching for the phone when the Reverend Charles Pinkney walked into the shop.

Reverend Pinkney was minister of the Warner Pier Non-Denominational Fellowship Church. I might have refused Amos Hart's invitation to sing in the church's choir, and I'd never attended services there, but I knew Reverend Pinkney by sight. As I say, Warner Pier is a small town.

Reverend Pinkney had been pointed out to me several times by several different people, usually with the words, "He's *my* preacher!" The identification always featured a heavy emphasis on the "my." Occasionally the report ended with the word "meant." As in, "I'm so glad I found *his* church. It was meant."

The "my preacher" and "his church" comments had led me to believe the Non-Denominational Fellowship Church centered on Reverend Pinkney. I'm not an expert on theology, but I always distrust churches built as personality cults. And the secondhand reports of his sermons seemed to reflect the view that if we do good and believe the correct theology, God will reward us with prosperity and happiness. This doesn't jibe with my observation that the most loving and faithful people around still have lots of troubles and woes. They usually just cope with them better. Anyway, I didn't think I'd fit into "his" church.

So I pretended to study my computer screen, but I confess that I was checking out Reverend Pinkney as he walked across the shop. He was a handsome man of around thirty, tall, with dark hair that had been expertly cut. He wore a puffy winter jacket that looked like the real thing—down stuffing rather than polyester—and he was carrying a large file folder. He smiled broadly as he spoke to the girl at the counter. I assumed he was buying chocolates. Then I realized that the counter girl was gesturing toward my office.

She called out, "Lee! Reverend Pinkney wants to talk to you."

I motioned to him and tried to smile. "Come in!" I kept my seat, determined that I would treat the fabled preacher as an ordinary caller. In fact, maybe I could pump him a bit—get some information about a couple of his parishioners, Mozelle and Amos Hart.

Reverend Pinkney came into my cubbyhole, smiling a toothy smile and holding out a hand. "Hi," he said. "I'm Chuck Pinkney, and I want to ask a favor."

I shook his hand. "What do you need?"

The Reverend Pinkney opened the large folder he was holding and pulled out a flyer for his church. "Could we post one of these in your window? We're having special services during WinterFest."

I looked at the flyer. Probably some church member had produced it on a home computer, but it was still slickly done, with four-color printing on good paper. It featured a photograph of the church with a family of happy snowmen on the front lawn. Not real snowmen. Plywood snowmen. Or maybe snow people, because two of them were women. And each fake snow person held a Bible. I could tell their books were Bibles, because they held them clutched to their snowy chests so that gold lettering reading "Holy Bible" was visible.

I usually turn down requests to hang stuff in our windows. I hate to see a shop window so cluttered that passersby can't see what's inside, and we already had two WinterFest posters up. As a committee member I hadn't felt I could refuse to hang those. But being cooperative might help me pump Reverend Pinkney.

Reverend Pinkney—Chuck—smiled winningly. "It will only be for ten days. The services are this Sunday and the next."

"Sure," I said. "You can put it up. Do you need tape?"

He produced a tape dispenser from his pocket. "I'm all set. And I'm glad to meet you, Lee. You're on the WinterFest committee, right?"

"I handle the money. Nothing creative. But I believe a couple of our committee members are in your congregation— Amos Hart and Mozelle French."

"Yes, Amos has been holding his chorale rehearsals in our church."

"The committee appreciates your support, Reverend Pinkney."

"Chuck. Please. And it's not my support." He grinned, displaying plenty of that old S.A., and I saw that his sex appeal might be one of the attractions of his church to the women members.

"It's not your support?"

"Use of the building is up to the church board, not the minister. They make the decisions."

"I hope that means the board has to come down in the evenings to let the singers in and out for rehearsal instead of sticking you with the job."

Reverend Pinkney—Chuck—laughed. "Amos has a key."

"He's on the staff, isn't he?"

"Yes and no. We can only afford to pay him in the summer, when our choir—and our congregation—is much larger than it is this time of the year. Our year-round staff is only me and two part-timers, a secretary and a custodian."

"He talks as if he's pretty active down there."

"Yes, Amos is on the board, and every Wednesday night he's there putting the choir through its paces."

"I guess he's been there even more lately, getting the chorale ready for its performance."

"I think they've rehearsed every night."

Had Amos been at the church the night Mendenhall was killed? "Oh? Did they rehearse Tuesday night?"

"I'm not sure. I don't think the chorus was there in the evening. The soloists were practicing Tuesday afternoon, so I got a preview."

"How did the soloists sound?"

"Great! Amos is a very good director, and he's recruited some fine singers. He's one of our church's most active laymen."

"It sounds as if Mozelle is also an active member."

"Definitely! Mozelle is currently our board chair." Chuck flashed those teeth again. "Do you and your husband have a church home, Mrs. Woodyard?"

"Please call me Lee, Chuck. And, no, we haven't quite settled that question, since we were brought up in different denominations."

Chuck responded with a one-paragraph wrap-up of the advantages of his church to couples like us, even producing a second, smaller flyer with the church's meeting times and phone numbers. It seemed Joe and I could each keep our core beliefs intact at Warner Pier Non-Denominational Fellowship. The Reverend Chuck Pinkney did his presentation well. He used words like "contemporary" and "spirit-filled." His brief description was obviously well-rehearsed.

When he stopped for a breath, I stood up. "That's interesting. Now, let's see about hanging those flyers."

Chuck smiled, but his smile had grown a little stiff. Had I snubbed his spiel? I hadn't intended to be rude. Trying to act friendly, I escorted him to the front of the shop and selected a spot for his flyer. He taped it in place, and I turned toward him, ready to shake hands and end our little interview.

Chuck took my hand, but instead of saying good-bye, he frowned and lowered his voice. "Mrs. Woodyard. Lee. I feel that I must say one thing to you."

"Certainly."

He seemed to find it hard to get the words out, but he finally managed. "Since you don't have a minister of your own . . . If you or your husband should find yourselves in need . . . I mean . . . Well . . . If I can be of service, please don't hesitate to call me." Then he almost ran out the front door.

I stood looking after him, perplexed. What was eating the man? Why did he think Joe and I might need pastoral care?

Then, behind me, I heard a whisper. "She's the one the waitress was talking about," it said.

I turned to see two women who were looking at everything in the shop except me. One was a bleached blonde and the other an overdyed brunette. I'd never seen either of them before. Tourists, I thought. Tourists drawn to Warner Pier for the WinterFest.

Had they been whispering about me? It didn't seem possible.

Then one of them—the blonde—sneaked a peek in my direction. When she saw me looking at her, she jumped and looked panicky.

They *had* been talking about me.

I slunk back to my office. Some waitress had told them about me. I was "the one." I didn't have to ask why I was being singled out.

I was the murder suspect. The probable killer.

And the Reverend Chuck Pinkney thought I might need

pastoral care. I eyed his flyer. Had he really wanted it in the window? Or had it been an excuse to come in and offer his services? Maybe he wanted a dramatic confession, one he could describe to television reporters.

I resisted the temptation to go back out into the shop and tear the flyer down. I turned back to my computer screen and pretended to read what was up on it.

But if I'd had a tablecloth handy, I'd have chewed it to shreds.

Chapter 12

That may have been the lowest moment in my whole life. As I sat there at the computer, I couldn't think of a lower one. I even ran a collection of low moments through my brain, trying to think of which was the worst. Only one came close.

When I left my first husband—Rich Godfrey—I didn't take my clothes, jewelry, or car. I even left behind the sheets and towels and dishes and pots and pans. And my checkbook and credit cards. I took nothing but a few clothes left from the time before I married Rich, and I talked my mom into letting me stay with her.

I left Rich because I had realized that he believed I'd married him for his money. I left everything behind because, naively, I thought that if I showed him I could live without the things he'd given me, he would understand that I married him because I loved him. I thought—like an idiot—that when Rich understood that I loved him for himself, not his money, our marriage would be magically healed. He would no longer regard me as something he owned, but as a life partner.

Ha.

What I came to understand—on my own; I didn't have the money or the time for a therapist—was that Rich didn't separate the objects he owned from himself. When I rejected his possessions, when I declined to be one of those possessions, I rejected him. My gesture left our marriage irretrievably broken.

The truth of the situation became clear to me a week after I'd moved out. The only job I could find on a moment's notice was waiting tables in a Mexican restaurant, and some of Rich's friends saw me there. One night shortly before closing, I got a phone call from the wife of one of them.

"Lee! It's Marilyn. Is it true that you left Rich for . . ." She named a name prominent in Dallas. I'll call him John Cowboy. As in Dallas Cowboy.

I was as stunned as if I'd been run over by the Cowboy line. I couldn't even answer. She finally spoke again. "Lee? Are you there?"

"I've never even met John Cowboy," I said. "Where did you hear that?"

"Well . . . Oh, you know . . ."

"I'm not dating anybody. Does Rich think I am?"

"He heard you were talking to John Cowboy at the restaurant."

"What does John Cowboy look like?"

"You don't even know what he looks like?"

"No. I never pay much attention to football. If I talked to John Cowboy, it was because he was a customer. And I've got to hang up now. One of my tables wants a check."

"Okay, Lee. But listen . . ." Marilyn lowered her voice. "Watch your step."

I didn't figure out her comment until a strange car parked down the street from my mother's place that night. Rich had hired private detectives. I was under surveillance.

He apparently thought that I wouldn't have left one wealthy man until I had another on the string. My dramatic gesture of leaving everything behind, meant to convince Rich that I wasn't interested in his money, had confused and infuriated him. So he was starting gossip about me. Hurtful gossip.

All I could hope was that John Cowboy would hear the rumors and knock Rich's block off.

I had always thought that was the lowest moment in my life. But now I'd reached an even lower one. Then I was the object of gossip about my marriage and my love life. Now people apparently were gossiping about whether I had killed two people.

I sat at my computer and had a real pity party. Poor little me. People were saying ugly things about me. Untrue things.

I guess I looked as if I'd had a shock, because Aunt Nettie came into my office. "What's wrong, Lee?"

I blew my nose and told her about the bleached blonde and the dyed brunette. People were talking about me.

"My grandma down in Texas would have said I feel so bad I ought to go out in the backyard and eat worms," I said.

"That's too bad." Aunt Nettie leaned toward me. "Do you want me to make you some chocolate worms?"

After I blinked a couple of times, I began to laugh.

Aunt Nettie spoke again. "The ground's frozen too hard to dig up regular worms, but I could make you some chocolate ones if you think eating a few would help the situation. Milk chocolate would probably look the most realistic."

"Okay, Aunt Nettie. I get the point."

"Do you? Lee, in this situation with Mendenhall—have you done anything you're ashamed of?"

"No, I haven't."

"I didn't think so. I think you did the best you could."

"So I'd better forget the Warner Pier gossips, right?"

"Right. You have more important things to worry about than what two tourists say." Aunt Nettie gave the word "tourists" that Warner Pier spin, a little undertone that puts them in their places. And their places are three steps behind locals—people who live and work in Warner Pier year-round—and two steps behind summer people—people who own cottages and whose families come to our area every year.

She got up. "So, I assume you and Joe will be at the play opening tonight."

"Oh, yes. I'll face gossip and exhaustion and amateur theatricals, but I'll be there. And so will Joe, even if I have to hog-tie him and throw him in the back of the pickup."

"You may have to pick me up. Hogan will probably be busy detecting."

I got back to work feeling less downhearted. At least Aunt Nettie didn't feel sorry for me.

After all, I reminded myself, when I realized that Rich had sicced private eyes on me, I had reacted aggressively. I found a lawyer who was willing to represent me on the chance that he'd collect a fee from Rich. Then I moved back to the town where I was born, Prairie Creek. My dad knew all the sheriff's deputies and town policemen, and Prairie Creek is so small that strangers stand out. My dad's pals ran the private eyes out of town fast.

After my lawyer threatened Rich with a slander suit, we were able to have a semicivilized divorce, though my attorney was mad because I continued to refuse a financial settlement. Rich was mad about it, too, if the truth is to be told, because he wanted to brag to his friends about how big a financial hickey I had given him. Rich did pay my lawyer, and in the end, I did keep some of my clothes—the ones I could wear to the office. I sent the rest to the resale shop and donated the proceeds to a women's shelter.

Reacting aggressively had worked that time, and I'd better use the same plan this time, I decided. I resolved to intensify the effort to check on which WinterFest committee members had received calls from Mendenhall.

I decided to talk to Sarajane, just casually. For that, I needed an excuse, and I thought I had one.

I pulled out the file that held current invoices and leafed through them. Aha. My memory was correct. On Monday Sarajane had called in an order for two pounds of crème de menthe bonbons ("The formal after-dinner mint.") for the Peach Street Bed and Breakfast Inn. Sarajane put one of these on each of her guests' pillows when she turned down the beds.

A check of the storeroom found the bonbons still sitting there in their box; she hadn't picked them up yet. I felt sure she'd appreciate it if I dropped them off on my way home.

Although Sarajane's bed and breakfast bore the name of one of Warner Pier's main streets, it wasn't in our downtown area. It was at the far end of Peach Street, in a secluded and heavily wooded area. There was plenty of room for a parking lot, a spacious terrace where she served summer guests wine and cheese, and even a gazebo with a chaise for lazy afternoons with a book. The inn was cozy in winter, too, when it featured a wonderful fireplace. In fact, it might be even better then, because the big tourist rush ended with Labor Day, so winter guests could have it almost to themselves. Except—or so we hoped—during the Winter Arts Festival.

The inn was decorated with country-style knickknacks. It had only a few guest suites, and Sarajane was able to run it by herself, if she needed to. The inn was so successful that she could sell out and retire to Florida any day she wanted to.

I left the office a little early, and it was just beginning to get dark as I turned into the gravel drive. I saw that Sarajane had joined in the snowman theme. Two round white figures on the porch wore battered hats and held brooms. I parked at the side of the big Victorian house, collected the crème de menthe bonbons, and followed the walk around to the back entrance. The back porch light wasn't on, but I had plenty of light to get up the steps.

I knocked at the door and was hit by spotlights. Four brilliant outdoor lights were trained at the back porch, and Sarajane—at least I assumed it was her—had turned them on.

I saw that the door was centered by a peephole, so I stepped back, making sure I was in view.

I heard scrabbling sounds from inside, and a voice hissed. I couldn't understand what it was saying. Still Sarajane didn't open the door. More hissing. Finally the door opened a crack.

"Hello, Lee," Sarajane said. "I wasn't expecting anyone."

"Sorry to surprise you." I held up the box of chocolates. "I was trying to get everything cleared away before the weekend rush started. So I'm delivering your chocolates."

"Thank you." Sarajane opened the door slightly and reached out for the box.

She wasn't going to invite me in. Darn. How could I question her while standing on the back porch? I thought quickly. "Sarajane, you served the most delicious spiced tea at your Thanksgiving open house. Do you give out that recipe?"

"I'll give you a jar of the mix." She opened the door, and I saw a back hall furnished with a bench, handy for pulling on snow boots, a hall tree hung with jackets, and a chest of drawers which could be used for storing scarves and gloves.

"You make that spiced tea from a mix?"

"I make the mix myself." Sarajane moved from the back hall to the kitchen. She opened a pantry door and took out a half-pint jar filled with powder. All the while she described what was in it—instant tea and lemonade among other things. She turned on all the lights in the kitchen. And she talked volubly about the spiced tea.

I had the feeling she was inviting me to take a look around. Why? Why had she hesitated to let me in, then made a show of letting me see the kitchen?

I had to get down to the real reason I came. "Sarajane, you tickled my curiosity, you know."

"How?"

"You mentioned that you'd made an 'emergency trip' to Wal-Mart Tuesday night. I wondered if you saw George there."

"George. George Jenkins?" Her voice had no inflection at all.

"Yes. He went to Wal-Mart Tuesday night, too. Maybe you ran into him."

"No. It's a big place. Though I admit it's rare that I go there without meeting someone from Warner Pier." Sarajane glanced at the clock on the wall over the sink.

I'd obviously outstayed my welcome. I thanked her for the spiced tea mix and moved toward the back door. "I hope you're enjoying your friend's visit."

"I'm sorry not to introduce her to you, Lee. She's been ill. She wanted some peace and quiet."

I had my hand on the door handle before I noticed that the top drawer in the dresser was open by several inches. And inside I could see a pistol.

I went out the door and down the steps and into the van in a flash. Then I laughed at myself. Sarajane had already told me she slept with a pistol beside her bed. Her B and B was in a lonely area. If she kept a weapon beside her bed at night, she'd probably also want it in a handy place when she wasn't in bed.

But why did she feel she had to have it available when she opened the back door? It wasn't dark yet. All she had to do was look out the side window to see me get out of my van. I didn't understand it. And who was the mysterious guest?

Joe had never answered my messages, but we got home almost at the same moment. He already knew about the skillet being found in the van. He'd spent the afternoon discussing that skillet with VanDam and McCullough.

Which meant he was in an even worse mood than I was. When I mentioned the play, he growled.

I tried psychology on him. "You can stay home if you want to," I said. "I'll pick up Aunt Nettie. We'll go together."

"You can't possibly want to go to an amateur play tonight."

"No, I don't want to, but I'm afraid I have to." I described the "She's the one" episode.

Joe's face screwed up. "Damn! Lee, I'm sorry."

"I gave myself a major pity party. Cried two Kleenexes sodden. Then Aunt Nettie told me to buck up, that I hadn't done anything wrong, and I shouldn't act as if I had. I decided she was right. If I creep around as if I'm afraid of talk, it will only make the whole situation worse."

Joe kissed me. He almost always knows the right thing to do. "You're right. We both need to go to that play. Have I got time for a shower?"

"If you don't bask too long. I'll get the dinner on the table. Then you can do the dishes while I get dressed. We need to pick up Aunt Nettie at seven thirty."

Aunt Nettie, Joe, and I were in the Warner Pier High School auditorium ten minutes before curtain time.

The WinterFest play was a community project, not a high school function, which was why the WinterFest budget included the auditorium rental we were trying to get underwritten. Warner Pier High School's auditorium is like every other high school auditorium in the country, I guess. The Warner Pier teams are called the Wolves, and the auditorium was decorated with that in mind. Big plywood cutouts with fierce, howling wolves painted on them usually flanked the stage.

Maggie had hidden the howling wolves with even larger plywood snowmen, and she'd turned the stage itself into a winter wonderland with rolls of cotton batting and glitter. A quaint chalet was painted on the backdrop.

No one openly shunned Joe and me as we came in. In fact, many of our friends clustered around us. I couldn't tell if they were defiant of public opinion, curious, or sincerely glad to see us.

Mozelle and Amos, openly together, came in right behind us, reminding me that I hadn't checked on their stories for Tuesday night. I'd given up all pretense at subtlety. So, once Amos wandered off to hang up their coats, I bluntly questioned Mozelle.

"Did Mendenhall call you Tuesday night?"

"I told you, Lee. My number wasn't on the list Mendenhall had."

"Oh, that's right. What were you doing that evening?"

Mozelle looked at me coldly. "I was in Chicago. I had dinner with some friends and spent the night at the Ritz-Carlton. It wasn't until the next morning that my business was resolved, and I decided I would be able to return for the WinterFest events."

"How about last night? Did you and Amos go out to dinner?"

"We did not. We'd both had plenty to eat at the reception. We went to Amos' house to listen to a wonderful new CD he had. The London Philharmonic."

She walked away.

We had to go to our seats then, and Maggie's play began. It was a whodunit, with characters drawn from classic mysteries—the stiff colonel, the innocent young girl, the rich uncle, the naive priest, and a half dozen others—all isolated in an Alpine ski lodge in a snowstorm. At the end of the first act, the characters were being terrorized by an obviously fake snowman whose head looked more like a marshmallow than a snowball and who lumbered around the stage on giant shoes like a clown might wear. Maggie hadn't been able to borrow one of the "real" snowmen mascots' outfits.

It was good fun, the kind of look at fictional murder that makes real-life crime seem less frightening. I felt better when we got up to stretch at the intermission. Then Joe wandered off, Aunt Nettie stopped to talk to Sarajane Harding, and I came face-to-face with Amos Hart.

He was wearing a bow tie embellished with tiny snowmen. He waved a plastic cup holding what looked like cranberry punch. "Very tasty."

"I'm sure it is," I said. "But I think I'll skip." I hate most kinds of fruit punch, but there was no need to explain that. Instead I bulled right in with my questions. "Amos, you never said—did Mendenhall call you Tuesday night?"

"I wasn't home, and I don't have an answering machine."

"Oh? Were you with Mozelle?" It wouldn't do any harm to check on Mozelle's alibi.

"No. She was in Chicago."

"Oh, yes! Now I remember. I've been asking so many people about Tuesday night that I get all mixed up."

"I did go by her house, because I'd promised to feed her cat. But that was before the chorus rehearsal."

"I thought the chorus rehearsed Tuesday afternoon."

Amos smiled patiently. "The soloists rehearsed Tuesday afternoon. We had sectional rehearsals Tuesday night."

Then he reached over and patted my hand. "Now, Lee, I know how worried you are about all this business with Mendenhall, about the tragedy of Mary Samson's death. But you'd be so much better off if you'd simply trust in the Lord."

I bit my tongue and did not say that I'd always heard that the Lord helped those who helped themselves.

Amos wasn't waiting for me to say anything, however. He went right on. "It's very hard for us to understand the Lord's will, but everything that happens is for the best."

Everything? Did that include Mary Samson's murder?

"Someday, maybe years from now, you'll see that everything happens for a reason. We have to accept the Lord's will."

That was when I blew up. "Amos," I said, "when I went to Sunday school, they told me that murder is definitely against God's will. 'Thou shalt not kill,' remember? You can accept what's happened to Mendenhall and to Mary Samson if you want to. But do not blame it on God. Personally, I intend to do all I can to see that the killer is brought to justice."

I resisted the temptation to snatch Amos' cranberry punch out of his hand and pour it down his shirtfront. Instead I turned and walked away. Luckily I found Joe and attached myself to his arm. Joe always has a calming effect on me.

Then I noticed that he was talking with the Reverend Chuck Pinkney.

Remembering how Reverend Pinkney and I had parted— with his offer of pastoral guidance—I almost jumped guiltily. But I managed to recover and pretend to be calm.

Chuck Pinkney then introduced me to an attractive and very pregnant companion. "My wife, Darla."

"How do you do, Darla." I said, determined to keep up the illusion that I had nothing on my mind but the Winter-Fest activities. "Are you enjoying the play?"

"Oh, yes. We all need a laugh these days, don't we?"

"I know I do."

Darla and I had exchanged two or three more similarly witty and intelligent remarks when Amos Hart and Mozelle French entered the periphery of my vision. They seemed to be intent on joining their pastor.

I started to move away, but before I could say good-bye, Darla Pinkney spoke. "Maybe I ought to get off my feet, Chuck."

Chuck gallantly took her arm and escorted her toward the auditorium.

Joe and I followed, but I don't think Darla knew quite

how close we were behind them. Just as we reached the door to the auditorium, she spoke to Chuck again. I could tell she was trying to speak quietly, but I heard her clearly.

"Sorry, but Mr. Blessed and Mrs. Assurance were headed toward us. I don't have the patience you do."

If Chuck replied, I didn't hear what he said. Maybe I was occupied with hiding a grin. "Mr. Blessed and Mrs. Assurance." A reference to an oversentimental old hymn, and the perfect description of Mozelle and Amos.

I felt myself warming toward Darla, and even toward Chuck. For the first time I considered that Amos' religiosity might not reflect his pastor's. In fact, it might be a real pain in the neck to his pastor.

We were drinking coffee at Aunt Nettie's house when Hogan came home. He looked even more tired than Joe had, and he hadn't had dinner. Nettie began to fix something for him, and Joe and I got up to say good-bye.

"See you round the cop shop," I said. "I guess I'm still suspect number one."

Joe and Hogan exchanged a look.

"Come on, guys," I said. "I can take it. I know Mc-Cullough thinks I killed Mendenhall."

"Actually . . ." Hogan spoke slowly. "Actually, Lee, when we found out how many phone calls Mendenhall made after he checked into the motel, you moved pretty far down the list. All those calls pretty well prove that he was alive after you dropped him off. Even McCullough can't see you running back to Lake Knapp an hour or two later to do him in."

"He thinks I killed Mendenhall," Joe said. "He thinks you killed Mary Samson."

"But that's ridiculous! Isn't he convinced by Hogan's idea about Mendenhall phoning for paid companionship?"

Hogan frowned. "The phone records don't back that up."

"You mean there's no such number on Mendenhall's phone? But what about the room phone?"

"None there."

"What about that sleazy desk clerk."

"He claims he never does such a thing. . . ."

"Oh, sure."

"He even offered his own cell phone to show that he hadn't made such a call Thursday night."

"How about the motel pay phone?"

"There isn't one." Hogan sighed. "Sorry, Lee, but there's no proof that Mendenhall called anyone on any phone except people on that list of WinterFest members."

German Chocolate Cake—yum, yum!

One of America's favorite desserts—Baker's German's Sweet Chocolate Cake—is neither "Baker's" nor "German's."

Commonly known as "German Chocolate Cake," this is a delicately flavored light chocolate cake made with a particular type of sweetened cooking chocolate. Between each of its three layers and on top is a caramel icing packed with pecans and coconut.

The "Baker's" in the cake's name came from the chocolate manufacturer, not because it's designed for the exclusive use of bakers.

The "German's" is from Sam German, a Baker's employee who came up with the sweet cooking chocolate in 1852.

At that time most chocolate was still used for making beverages, but the Baker's company published a twelve-page booklet of baking recipes in 1870. German Chocolate Cake, however, was not in the booklet.

German Chocolate Cake was apparently invented by a Texas woman who submitted it to a Dallas newspaper in 1957. She named the cake after the chocolate she used to make it, and it swept the nation.

Chapter 13

There didn't seem to be any more to say. Apparently neither Joe nor I faced immediate arrest—probably because Alex VanDam knew us well enough to think we weren't very likely candidates as murderers.

But he wasn't in charge of the Lake Knapp end of the investigation. McCullough was, and he must have decided that while neither of us could have killed both Mendenhall and Mary Samson, we could each have killed one of them and helped the other cover up the crime.

He could give us a lot of grief. He'd already warned me he could make me sorry. I shuddered as I remembered his words. "I can throw you to the wolves anytime I want to."

Anyway, I wouldn't say I slept real well that night, and I had a hard time dragging myself into the office the next morning. It was Saturday, but we would be open all day because of the WinterFest promotion.

As I went into the shop, ready to open the front door for customers, I remember thinking, "At least things can't get much worse."

I was wrong. When I opened the door, one of those wolves McCullough had threatened me with was right outside.

I didn't recognize that first wolf, but I felt as though I

ought to. He was good-looking, with dark hair cut fashionably, and he was familiar, though I couldn't remember why. But I'm a Texan, and we're brought up to be friendly, so I greeted him like a long-lost pal. Or an important customer.

"Hi, there," I said, smiling brightly. "Nice to see you. Come on in."

He had a toothy, lobolike smile. When he spoke, his voice was mellow. "You're Mrs. Woodyard."

That remark told me I didn't know him well, but it still seemed as if I ought to recognize him.

"Yes, I'm Lee Woodyard. I'm sorry. I've forgotten your name." I stuck out my hand.

He shook my hand, and his grin became even toothier. "I'm Gordon Hitchcock. LMTV news. I wanted to bring you a videotape of all our coverage of the Winter Festival."

Oh, Lordy! I'd never met this guy. He seemed familiar because I'd seen him on one of the Grand Rapids television stations.

I yanked my hand away and stepped back, ready to refuse to answer questions. I knew enough to be wary of television reporters bearing gift tapes. Could I order him out of the shop?

It was too late. Gordon Hitchcock was inside; he strolled over to the counter and casually laid the tape down beside the cash register.

"Sometimes a tape like that can help committees get grants for future projects," he said. "We've tried to help your project. In fact, we ran a long interview with your spokeswoman."

"Mozelle French? Yes, I believe I saw it."

"In fact, we ran that interview twice. At least, excerpts from it ran again last Tuesday."

"Thanks for bringing the tape," I said. "But you should take it to Ramona VanWinkle-Snow, our chair. She's right down the street at Snow Photography."

"Sergeant McCullough suggested that I talk to you. And a chocolate shop is so much more fun to visit than a photography studio is."

Gordon Hitchcock might be a wolf, but he was using only the best butter. He'd approached me in a way, with a gift and a compliment, that would hardly let me toss him out of the shop. I decided I'd better try my own best butter on him. I'd be friendly, but I wouldn't talk about anything but chocolate.

"TenHuis Chocolade is very proud of our product," I said. "Let me give you a sample."

"You don't need to."

"All visitors to TenHuis Chocolade get a bonbon or a truffle." I walked behind the counter. "You look like a Jamaican rum kind of guy. That's an all-dark chocolate bonbon. Or would you prefer Baileys Irish Cream? A dark chocolate bonbon with a classic cream liqueur interior. If you like milk chocolate, I can recommend the coffee truffle. Milk chocolate inside and out, flavored with Caribbean coffee."

"I had a few questions about these killings, Mrs. Woodyard. You knew both Dr. Fletcher Mendenhall and Mary Samson."

"Sorry. I can't talk about that. Maybe you'd like to try a strawberry truffle. The interior is white chocolate flavored with real strawberries, and it's coated with dark chocolate."

"Sergeant McCullough says you have been questioned about the killings several times."

"My husband and I are cooperating with the investigating officers in any way we can. But if you want a statement, you'd better talk to Sergeant McCullough or to Lieutenant VanDam of the state police." I gave him a smile that matched his, tooth for tooth. "All I do is sell chocolate."

I don't know if Hitchcock gave a signal of some sort or what, but the door to the shop opened again, and a scrawny guy came in. On his shoulder he was holding a camera, which he aimed like a bazooka. I almost expected flames to shoot out of it.

I swallowed a growl and smiled at the second wolf. "Oh, good! You're going to take some pictures of our marvelous chocolates. We're very proud of them. Here, have a sample." I reached into the case and brought out a mocha pyramid, then held it toward the camera. "This features a milky coffee-flavored interior enrobed in dark chocolate and formed into a pyramid. The ancient Egyptians never had anything like this! But maybe the ancient Aztecs did; after all, they also built pyramids. The Aztecs used cacao beans for money as well as for making chocolate drinks!"

I went on talking inanely about chocolate—"The emperor Montezuma supposedly drank chocolate before he visited his harem, you know"—and Hitchcock kept asking me questions about the murders.

"Were you the last person to see Professor Mendenhall?"

"I don't know about that. But I do know that chocolate houses were centers of political discussion in seventeenth-century England."

I didn't see how he was going to get anything usable out of my stupid remarks, but he scared me. I felt extremely relieved when he finally said, "Well, I guess you're not going to tell us anything, Mrs. Woodyard."

I smiled, thinking he was going to leave. "Oh, I can talk about chocolate all day long."

And then he zinged me. "Yeah. You obviously care a lot about chocolate. But I guess you just don't care a lot about Mary Samson."

Stabbed. Right through the heart.

I lost it. "Listen, bud," I said, "Mary Samson was as sweet, shy, and kind a person as anyone who ever lived. She was killed in a cruel way. I'm not going to sensationalize her death so you can increase your ratings. Please leave."

I folded my arms and closed my mouth. I tried to give Gordon Hitchcock and his cameraman my stoniest stare. Unfortunately, my eyes began to fill up, which pretty much ruined the effect. I turned away and walked toward the workshop. For the first time I realized Aunt Nettie was standing in the doorway.

I was afraid she would give me a hug or do something else to try to comfort me. And that would look as if we were putting on a show, exploiting Mary Samson's death just the way I had accused Gordon Hitchcock of doing.

But Aunt Nettie didn't even look at me as I passed her. She walked toward the television reporters. "This is a place of business," she said calmly. "My niece and I are extremely upset about the death of our friend, but we have to carry on our business. Please leave."

I don't know if Gordon Hitchcock had any shame or not, but his cameraman apparently did. He lowered his weapon—I mean, his camera. "Come on, Gordie," he said. Then he went out the front door. I guess Gordon followed him. I didn't look back.

I kept walking until I was in our break room. I grabbed up a Kleenex from the box Aunt Nettie kept next to the microwave and wiped my eyes.

Then I thought about Joe. I had to warn him. Joe had a dread of the press, a reaction to the way the tabloids had covered his first marriage and the way they'd covered his divorce. He definitely would not like Gordon Hitchcock and his cameraman, or any other reporter, to drop in at his boat shop.

I snatched up the telephone, called Joe, and warned him about my run-in with the Grand Rapids television newsman.

"It's that blankety-blank McCullough," I said. "He threatened to 'throw me to the wolves.' And that's just what he's done."

"You're probably right," Joe said. "I guess we'd both better hide out today."

"Should we ask Webb what he recommends?"

He thought a moment. "Let me think up a press release. I'll call you right back. And I'll let Webb know what's going on, but we might not want to tell the general public we've consulted a lawyer."

I hung up and began moving my theater of operations from my glass-walled office near the front door to our more secluded break room. Luckily my laptop was at the office, so I was able to move it to the back of the building and still access my e-mail, accounting files, and other computer business from a spot where people entering the shop could not see me.

I was almost set up when Joe called back. He dictated a simple press release, in which the two of us denied any additional knowledge about the killings of Mendenhall and Mary Samson and pledged all possible cooperation to the "proper authorities." I typed it out and printed up twenty-five copies. We put a stack in the shop, and the counter girls were instructed to hand them out to anybody who came in with a notebook or camera. They were told that I was unavailable to anybody who wasn't local. Dolly Jolly and Aunt Nettie were assigned to answer the telephone.

Then, marooned in the back room, I tried to get my work done without interfering with the coffee breaks and lunch hours of our staff. On a Saturday later in the winter, of course, we would have had only a few people there. Because it was the Christmas rush and the week of WinterFest, we had about twenty. I was definitely in their way.

Joe snuck in the back door at noon with two salami sandwiches and some potato chips. While we ate I worked on my chart of the WinterFest committee members and their whereabouts at the time Fletcher Mendenhall was killed. It wasn't very conclusive. Only Ramona, Amos Hart, and George Jenkins appeared to have alibis, and they could prove their whereabouts only during the early part of the evening.

"And Ramona and George claim they were together when Mary was killed," I said. "That doesn't exactly clear them."

"Why not?"

"If McCullough can think you and I colluded to kill two people, why should they be exempt from the same suspicion?"

"They're not married to each other."

"True. But it seems ridiculous to suspect anybody on this committee of doing anything violent. So we might as well suspect Ramona and George. Neither of them has a real alibi. They're no sillier than anyone else in the roles of suspects."

Joe laughed. "You're right. The whole situation is ridiculous. Mendenhall was killed because he was a drunk? Mary because she was too shy to open her mouth? It's stupid."

"Actually, I question Amos Hart's alibi, as well."

"Why?

"He says he was rehearsing the choir. But Reverend Chuck Pinkney says they had rehearsal in the afternoon. He didn't mention the evening. Amos claims the soloists rehearsed in the afternoon and the whole choir in the evening. He says they had sectional rehearsals."

"What are sectional rehearsals?"

"That's when the sopranos, altos, tenors, and basses practice their parts without the other sections present."

"Oh. That would be easy to check. Call Lindy."

Well, yeah. My best friend was a member of the Winter-Fest Chorus. She answered her cell phone on the first ring. Yes, she said, the WinterFest chorus had practiced in the evening. And, yes, Amos Hart had been there.

"Matilda VanDrusen led the sopranos," she said. "But Amos was around. I know I saw him just after I got there."

I hung up and repeated what she'd said to Joe. "By the time

Amos led the rehearsal and fed Mozelle's cat, his evening is pretty much taken up. It would be after ten o'clock before he could get up to Lake Knapp. What time did Mendenhall die?"

"I don't think the medical examiner has made a firm report yet, but ten o'clock seems pretty late. How about Mozelle? You didn't say anything about her."

"She wasn't on the list of WinterFest committee members, so Mendenhall didn't have her phone number. Apparently there's no call to her number on his cell phone. Plus, she says she was in Chicago. I guess Hogan or VanDam has checked up on that. Not that I wouldn't love to destroy her alibi."

Joe laughed. "I guess we all like to see pride taking a fall."

"Yep. But if Mozelle wasn't in Chicago, it will be up to Hogan to find it out. I guess all of this is for Hogan and Alex VanDam to find out. I'd better trust them to handle it."

We left it like that. I felt quite helpless about the whole situation. Here I was, hiding in the back room of TenHuis Chocolade, afraid to answer the phone, dreading going home—where Joe and I could easily be surrounded by the press.

I kept trying to get through that ghastly day. It was hard to do routine chores when I would rather have had a nervous breakdown. But I kept on keeping on, and eventually the sun went down, and the day ended. The candy-making ladies took off their hairnets and went home at four thirty. The counter girls locked the front door at five thirty. They pulled the shades, so I was able to leave my exile in the break room to help them clean the shop and prepare it for Sunday, when we would open at eleven a.m. We restocked the counter, swept the floor, and washed the fingerprints off the showcases. A few people knocked at the door, but we ignored them.

Then the girls got their coats, I unlocked the front door and opened it a crack so one of them could take a look outside to make sure the coast was clear before they sprinted for their cars. As the door opened, a folded piece of paper fell inside.

I picked it up warily, expecting to find a nasty note from Gordon Hitchcock or one of his fellow newshounds. But the note was from Jason Foster.

"Yikes!" I said. "If Jason came by, we should have let him in."

The note was hand-printed on paper torn from a lined yellow tablet.

> Hey, Lee! You're so hassled I don't blame you for not answering the door. I have an emergency request, and if you can't handle it, I'll understand.
>
> The West Michigan Tourism Council is coming tomorrow to check out WinterFest. They're meeting for breakfast at Warner Point at ten a.m. Do you have any of the ten-inch snowmen? I'd like to use ten of them for centerpieces.
>
> The bad news is we're starting to set up at seven a.m., and I'd need them before that. You'll have to bring them to the front door.
>
> Sorry to be a pain.
>
> Jason

I was tired, and I wanted to go home—even if that home turned out to be haunted by reporters and photographers. But there was no way I could turn down Jason's request. First, he was a friend, and you don't let your friends down. Second, for a merchant in Warner Pier, the West Michigan Tourism Council was a big deal. I could get a lot of business from the members—if they were impressed with our product. I resolved not only to find ten snowmen, but to send along several dozen two-piece boxes of TenHuis bonbons and truffles as little gifts for the council members.

So I shooed the counter girls out, then began packing up chocolate. Luckily there were plenty of snowmen and we had lots of two-piece boxes ready, some in seasonal colors and others in the standard TenHuis box, white with blue ribbon. But ten snowmen, each weighing a pound and a half, made two sizable boxes, mainly because each snowman required so much packing material to keep it safe. I used our sturdiest boxes and tied each box up with string so that it had a handle. The two-piece boxes weighed only an ounce each, but since three dozen of them meant thirty-six tiny boxes—each box roughly three inches long, an inch and a half wide, and an inch and a quarter tall—they filled several smaller boxes. I put those in a plastic sack and tied the top so that it had a handle, too.

I loaded all the chocolate into my van, then went home. I was relieved to find that no reporters were lying in wait. I carried the chocolate inside so it wouldn't freeze, and put it in the back hall so it wouldn't get too hot. Joe had fixed his usual dinner of frozen lasagna and bagged salad, and that night it looked good. After we ate I stood in the shower for half an hour. Then I got in bed and put my arms around the best-looking guy in west Michigan. He responded in a suitable manner.

At six fifteen the next morning, I hit my alarm at the first tinkle, trying not to wake Joe up. It was Sunday morning, after all, and as I had told Chuck Pinkney, we weren't regular churchgoers.

I didn't make coffee. I figured it would take only thirty minutes to deliver those chocolates to Warner Point. Maybe I'd stop at the doughnut shop on the way back and save myself the trouble of putting the cereal box on the table.

It was, of course, still pitch-dark as I turned onto the Warner Point driveway at six forty-five. The gated entry that the property had had when it was owned by Clementine Ripley was no longer there, and I could see the lights of the main building. The silly-looking snowman still stood near the wide front door. It had snowed lightly overnight, and a dusting of white covered the broad stone steps.

I parked the van on the semicircular drive, put my car keys in my jeans pocket, and got out. I wondered idly why Jason wanted me to bring the chocolates in the front door. Ordinarily deliveries would be made directly to the kitchen. But I didn't wonder about it too much. I simply popped the rear door of the van, pulled out the two heavy boxes of snowmen, and picked up the lighter but equally bulky sack of two-piece boxes. The handles I had tied meant I was able to carry all of them, though I had to leave my purse in the van. Then I walked up the steps, past the giant snowman, and knocked on the door.

There was no reaction. I didn't hear anybody moving inside. Maybe I should go around to the back. But Jason had specifically said come to the front.

I knocked again. Still no answer.

The keypad that opened the restaurant's front door was staring me in the face. I'm not a number person for nothing. Of course, Jason had probably changed the code since the days when Joe and I used to come by and check on the property. . . .

It was worth a try. I reached for the keypad and punched in the four magic numbers.

But before I could try the handle, something moved in the corner of my eye. I turned to see what it was.

The big, silly snowman was moving toward me. And he was swinging his snow shovel above his head.

Chapter 14

I hit the snowman with twenty pounds of chocolate.

That wouldn't have done him much harm if the chocolate hadn't been in two solid cardboard boxes with sharp corners, and if the snowman hadn't been standing on the snow-covered flagstone steps of Warner Point. But luckily the chocolate boxes actually were heavy and solid and had sharp corners. And the snowman was really standing on those steps, and the flagstones were covered with a light layer of snow. The combination meant my attack had more impact than might have been expected.

The snowman dodged to avoid my blow and dodging made his foot slip. His snow shovel descended through the air like some sort of enormous fan, but it missed me. I swung my boxes wildly one more time. I hit him in the head, and his feet went out from under him. He fell over backward, landing hard on his rump.

Now what should I do? The snowman was already scrambling around, trying to get to its feet. I couldn't rely on two boxes and a plastic sack of chocolate to be effective weapons for another attack. I had to get away.

I jumped around mentally—and probably physically. How could I escape? Should I get in the van? No. The back deck was still gaping open, and I'd turned off the motor and put the ignition key in the pocket of my jeans. By the time I could get in the driver's seat, dig out that key, and lock the doors—well, I just didn't have time to do that before the snowman climbed in through the back deck. And if I stopped to slam the back deck, I wouldn't have time to get in the van, dig out the key, and start the engine.

Should I run for the front gate? It was a long way away—like half a block—and I'd be in full view of the snowman all the way. That didn't seem to be a good idea. What if he had a gun? What if he could run faster than I could?

And even if I got out the front gate without being caught or shot, I'd still be running along an open road for between a quarter and a half a mile before I could reach a house, which might be an empty summer cottage.

My cell phone was in my purse on the floor of the van's front seat. And besides, Warner Point was a dead zone for cell phones. I had no quick way to call for help.

While my mind was analyzing the possible escape routes, my feet had already taken off running. They had decided that the smartest thing I could do was get out of sight as quickly as possible. They jumped down the steps and ran past the snow-man, on a path parallel to the front of the building. When I figured out where my feet were taking me, I realized my aim was to get around the corner, where I could dodge into some landscaping.

This seemed to be as good an idea as any. I was somewhat familiar with the terrain at Warner Point, and the snowman might not be. Besides, as soon as I got off those front steps, where the outdoor light was shining, it was still night.

I pounded along the driveway for thirty feet or so. Then I cut diagonally across the snow-covered lawn. The snow was deeper there, but that early in the winter, it wasn't too awfully deep. I lifted my feet up high and ran like a marching gazelle, past the banks of French doors that lined the main dining room.

When I got to the corner of the building, I swung around it without pausing. There were banks of shrubbery at that end—the west end—and I jumped into them. It was dark back there. The light from the porch was now fifty or sixty feet away and around a corner. I nestled into the dark and inched along the wall, moving toward the back of the building.

When I found myself behind a big evergreen, I stopped moving. I stood behind it, my back to the stone wall. I stayed still, or as still as I could with my knees knocking.

There was no sign of sunrise yet. It was very dark. I was well away of Warner Point's only outside light, but I was still afraid I might be easy to see because the snow on the ground and on the trees made everything brighter. I was wearing my red ski jacket. Would it look dark in the predawn duskiness? Or would it stick out like a poinsettia tossed into a snowbank? Would my white knit cap blend with the snow on the evergreen? Or would it stand out against the shrub like a snowball in a coal bin?

Before I could decide if my hidey-hole was safe or not, the snowman appeared. I could see him through the branches of the evergreen, but I could only hope he couldn't see me.

Actually, I could barely see him. It was that dark. Even though I had expected him to appear, all I could make out was a sort of general movement, a blob of white moving against the snow and the darker trees.

I held my breath. Then I saw a flash of light.

Damn! The snowman had a flashlight. If he turned it toward me, that red jacket was going to leap into his view.

But he didn't splash the light around. He kept it on the ground. I realized he was following my footprints.

I couldn't let him trap me between the evergreen and the wall of the building. I had to move.

Again the possibility that the snowman might have a gun hit me like a chunk of ice in the midriff. Then I told myself that was silly. If he'd had a gun, why would he have tried to hit me with a shovel?

Was he carrying the shovel now? I peered through the branches of the evergreen. I thought I saw the handle of the shovel. If he had the snow shovel in one hand and a flashlight in the other, I told myself, the only way he could be carrying a pistol would be in his teeth. Not too likely. Unless he had it in his pocket.

I began to edge along the wall, toward the back of the building.

As I moved, my sheltering evergreen shuddered all over. I froze. Would the snowman see the motion? Would it reveal where I was?

I couldn't tell what the creature was doing. I just knew I couldn't stay where I was. I kept edging along the side of the building behind the bushes, trying to watch the giant snowman as I moved. But I could see hardly anything except a quick blast of light from his flashlight now and then.

Why didn't he simply turn the darn thing on? Was he afraid that someone driving down the road would see a flash of light where none should be? I didn't understand what he was doing, but I was grateful he wasn't searching the bushes for me.

I kept moving along, trying to keep ahead of the thing following me. Then I turned the next corner, and there were no more bushes to hide behind. I'd reached the big terrace outside the main dining room.

The terrace was a broad expanse of flagstones. Jason used it for cocktail parties and extra seating in the summer. Now it was empty. Its tables, chairs, and umbrellas had been stored away, tucked in for the winter in some storage shed. It was surrounded by a low stone wall, and a smoothly manicured lawn—now covered with snow—grew right up to that wall.

At the opposite end of the terrace was an evergreen hedge, a hedge that blocked any view of what was behind it. I'd been around Warner Point enough to know what was there, however; behind the hedge was a fence, and behind the fence was the kitchen entrance to the restaurant. If there was anybody at the restaurant, the kitchen was where they'd be, getting ready for the big brunch. I could pound on the door and scream. There was a chance someone would hear me.

Like the main entrance, the kitchen entrance had a door with a keypad. If I got there, and nobody was inside, maybe—if I was lucky—the code I had in my head would open that door.

But to get to the kitchen door, I had to cross that broad terrace and get around that hedge. And there was no cover, no friendly shrubbery I could hide behind.

But I couldn't stay where I was, crouched behind the last bush on the west side of the building.

I took a deep breath and ran. I didn't try to climb over the little stone wall. I detoured around it. The snow was deeper out on the lawn. I did my marching gazelle act again, picking up my knees in a gait that must have looked as ridiculous as doing it felt.

I could hear the squeak of steps behind me, but I kept running. I slipped in the snow, but I kept running. I tripped over something—I had no idea what it was—but I didn't fall, and I kept running.

I passed the terrace, and I swung around the hedge. And I almost fell flat. I'd been running through snow, but the walk behind the hedge had been shoveled, so it had only a light covering of snow, the dusting that had fallen overnight. My gazelle gait didn't work there. I slid, but I caught myself against the fence, and I kept going for that back door.

There was a light over it, and the light was on. But when I

pounded on the door, no one answered. There was a window, but the light inside was dim, a night-light of some sort.

The keypad. I had to try the keypad. I punched in the numbers that I remembered from the times I'd seen Joe use them, and I hit ENTER. I turned the handle.

It didn't respond. The door stayed locked. Had I used the wrong numbers?

Frantically, I punched them in again. Again the handle wouldn't move. I tried a third time, leaning over to make sure I was touching the right series of numbers, pressing each button firmly.

The handle stayed solid. It did not turn.

The door was not going to open. And I was trapped in a narrow passageway with a solid fence on one side and a wing of the building on the other.

I bolted back the way I'd come. When I got to the end of it, I looked left. The snowman wasn't twenty feet away. He threw the snow shovel at me.

It missed. I screamed.

Then I ran to my right. I crossed the service drive—it had been plowed, but I skidded in the new layer of snow that covered the concrete. Then I cut left, out into the snow-covered grounds of Warner Point.

As I ran, I cursed Clementine Ripley's architect. Oh, I'd cursed Clementine Ripley many a time for the mean things she did to Joe, but this was the first time I'd cursed the architect who had designed her Warner Point house.

I cursed him because Warner Point is not built like a normal building. It's not a big rectangular block. No, Warner Point is like a series of buildings held together by glass corridors that go off in several directions. I'd run around the easy part; running around the rest of it would be like tracing the outline of a spider in the snow. The structure had long legs with buildings at the ends.

So I took off across the snow, trying to judge—in the dadgum dark—just how far I'd have to go to get around the east end of the dadgum building. There was no other direction to go. If I ran out into the woods, I'd soon come to Lake Michigan or to the Warner River or to the high stone wall Clementine Ripley had built to keep out the curious. Now it would keep me in.

So I cursed that architect and ran on past that wall of glass. That particular corridor led, I knew, to a building Clementine had used as a guest house. The corridor was about fifty feet long, but I'll swear that I ran at least five hundred feet to get past it. I could see the glass that lined it glinting. I couldn't see much, but when the glinting stopped I knew I'd come to the small stone building that held four guest suites—two upstairs and two down. I moved over next to the wall and felt my way to the corner of the building. As soon as I was around that corner, I dropped to my knees—don't ask me why—and looked back the way I'd come, toward the main building and the terrace.

There was no light, true, except for the little that leaked from the industrial lamp over the kitchen door. But there were no big trees in that area either.

Nothing was moving out there.

I knelt there, squinting my eyes, looking everywhere for that nightmarish snowman.

And far away, on the other side of the building, I heard a car's engine start up. The sounds of the motor grew a bit louder; then they faded away behind me.

A car had started up on the part of the drive on the east side of the house. And the car had driven away, apparently leaving the grounds.

Did I dare hope that the snowman had given up?

I got to my feet, and for the first time, I realized that I was still holding all that chocolate. I'd run through all that snow clutching about twenty pounds of chocolate.

I decided I could carry my sacks a little farther. I walked on around the guest house, peeking around the corners before I ventured out onto a new side. I made a wide circuit around the whole Warner Point building, being careful not to get close to a bush, a fence, or any other place where someone could be waiting in ambush.

When I got to the other end of the service drive—it wound all over the place before it got to that kitchen area where I'd crossed it earlier—I was able to see that a car had parked there and had recently driven off. I was careful not to step in the tracks of its tires, but they were not very distinct.

I followed the drive on around to the front of the house, eventually coming out on the circular drive where I'd started. I could see my van, still standing there with the back hatch gaping open.

I stood at the corner of the building for a long time, looking the scene over. There was light, of course, from that lone lamp at the entrance to the restaurant. The scene was absolutely still. Not a breeze ruffled a bush. Not an animal moved. No owls swooped through the trees.

That van stood there, enticing me, luring me. It had a heater, and I was really cold. It had locks on the doors. I could get inside, slam those doors, and be safe. I could start the motor and get the hell out of there.

Slowly I approached the van. Still nothing moved.

I walked up to the back and slammed the rear door.

The noise made me jump, but nothing else moved. I walked around to the driver's side, and I opened the door.

The snowman loomed up on the other side of the window.

I shrieked.

He was reaching for me.

I was running.

He cut me off, boxed me in between the van and the house.

He came nearer. He had that shovel.

I screamed and screamed again, but I had to back up. I felt the flagstone steps behind me.

He was forcing me up them. In another few steps, I'd be pinned against the building.

I reached the door. I began to beat on it helplessly.

I looked around. He raised the snow shovel.

I threw the boxes of chocolates at him.

One of the boxes hit him right in the face, right in the grinning mouth I knew was actually his eyehole. He stumbled.

Behind my back, I clutched at the door handle.

And it moved. The door opened, and I fell inside.

Chapter 15

I guess the sack of chocolates saved me. If I hadn't thrown it, the snowman wouldn't have stumbled. If he hadn't stumbled, he would have come right in that door after me.

But he did stumble, and I was able to kick the door shut before he could get to it.

I heard the lock click. I was inside, behind a heavy metal door, and the snowman was outside. I lay on the floor and shook.

But I didn't lie there more than a few seconds. There was always the chance that that snowman could get inside, too. Warner Point was lined with windows, some of them easy to kick out.

I crawled across the entrance hall and found the door to the dining room. Once inside, I stood up and felt my way toward the kitchen, bumping into tables and chairs in the dark.

Then an unearthly clamor broke out.

For a moment I thought Lake Michigan had developed a tsunami, it was on its way inland, and somebody was sounding the alarm. Then I realized the Warner Point burglar alarm had gone off.

I had no idea of the code needed to turn it off, and I didn't even know where to find the magic keypad that would do that. But I didn't care. The burglar alarm would call the security company, and the security company would call Jason and the Warner Pier Police Department, which was what I was trying to do anyway. Someone would be there to turn the darn thing off soon. And in the meantime, the clanging might scare the snowman away.

I kept feeling my way across the room, with the alarm ringing madly. I was sure there would be a light switch near the door into the kitchen, and I was right. I turned the lights on in the dining room and the kitchen. The lighted rooms were the most beautiful sight I'd seen in forever. Then I brought a dining room chair into the kitchen, because I figured the person who answered the alarm would come to the back door. And I sat down, with the alarm buffeting me with sound.

Soon I saw headlights flash outside the kitchen window. Someone had arrived. I considered opening the back door and coming out with my hands up. But that seemed a little risky; I didn't want to escape the ghastly snowman only to be shot by some trigger-happy security guard who thought I was a burglar.

When a face appeared at the back window, I was relieved to see that it was topped by a furry hat with a badge on the front. I kept sitting in my chair, with my hands in plain sight. In a moment the door opened, and Jerry Cherry, one of Warner Pier's patrolmen, came in.

I could have hugged his neck, but I just waved.

He looked at me and shook his head slowly. Then he referred to a notebook and went into what looked like a broom closet. In a few seconds, the raucous clang of the alarm stopped, and Jerry came out.

"Well, Lee," he said, "what are you up to this time?"

"It's a long story, Jerry, but if you saw a great big snowman loping across the drifts as you drove in, I'm willing to file a complaint accusing him of scaring the stuffing out of me."

I quickly told Jerry that I'd been chased by someone wearing the head of the snowman that decorated the Warner Point entrance porch.

"He tried to hit me with that snow shovel the snowman carries," I said. "When I managed to get inside, he must have run off. I expect he's long gone by now."

"We'll look for him." Jerry spoke into his radio, calling for backup and instructing the dispatcher to spread the word among other law enforcement people, telling them to stop anybody they found either driving or walking near Warner Point, even if the person wasn't wearing a snowman head.

By then more headlights were flashing outside, and in a moment Jason Foster walked through the back door. "I'm going to get that alarm yanked out of here," he said. "I'm sick and tired of having to come out at the crack of dawn because a cat ran over the terrace."

Then he stopped and stared at me. "Lee? How did you get here?"

"It's a long story," I said. "And I have a piece of advice for you."

"What's that?"

"Reprogram your front door."

"Front door? But we never come in that way. I don't even know how to open it from the outside."

"Luckily," I said, "I do." I got up and got a paper towel from a roll near the sink. All of a sudden my eyes were brimming. I turned to Jerry. "May I call Joe?"

Gradually things were sorted out.

Joe came. He'd been calling my cell phone, trying to figure out why a thirty-minute errand was taking an hour.

Jason assured me that the note stuffed through the door

of TenHuis Chocolade, asking for a special order of chocolate snowmen, had not come from him. He had not had an unexpected request for brunch for the West Michigan Tourism Council, so he hadn't needed to open early.

"I only wish they'd drop by," he said. "That would be very nice."

Of course, I'd already figured this out during my trudge around Warner Point in the snow. Jason fixed breakfast for all of us, however, and that was good.

Hogan came, listened to my story, and patted my hand. He said the head of the snowman had been found in the center of the circular drive. There were lots of tracks, both mine and some unidentified person with a foot a bit larger than mine. The crime lab would be there to look at them.

Alex VanDam came, listened to my story, and declared the grounds of Warner Point a crime scene. He told Jason he could plan on opening the restaurant for dinner, however.

Sergeant McCullough of the Lake Knapp PD came. He and Hogan and Alex VanDam went into the dining room and had a big argument. I overheard phrases like "pulling the wool" from McCullough, and like "a hard head and a closed mind" from Hogan. VanDam didn't say a lot.

I gathered that McCullough admitted the tracks in the snow showed I'd done a lot of running and tramping around outside and that somebody else had been right after me. But he thought Joe could have been the "snowman" who chased me. In other words, he was clinging to the theory that Joe and I could have combined forces to commit two murders. The excitement at Warner Point, in his opinion, was simply a distraction we'd planned to throw off the investigators.

Joe and I stayed out of it, except that Joe offered to give them some sample footprints. In a while VanDam came and told us we could go home. "We'll have a patrol car in your vicinity," he said.

I hadn't been a whole lot of help. Whenever I'd seen the snowman, I'd been running away from him in the dark. I'd never gotten a good look at him.

Of course, the person who had attacked me with the snow shovel and who chased me wasn't wearing the entire snowman mascot outfit. He'd simply stuck the head on. I did know that his body had not been unusually round, puffy, and snowmanlike. He'd been wearing something light colored, but it could have been khaki pants and a poplin jacket. Or a white ski jacket with light blue snow pants. I didn't have a clue. But he didn't have a limp, a peg leg, or any other physical characteristic I'd been able to identify. The big head even made it impossible for me to guess at his height.

I was relieved to find that he hadn't taken my purse or my phone from my van, which had been sitting there wide-open during the whole episode. I told Joe that after we got home.

"At least he didn't steal the van," I said. "But I wish I'd gotten a better look at him. I thought he was a giant, but that was probably because of the head. And my terror."

"I'm afraid it must have been someone you know," Joe said.

"Yeah. He wouldn't have bothered to disguise himself if he didn't think I might recognize him."

And that was the most important deduction we made.

Aunt Nettie met us at the house. She said she wanted to make sure I was all right. I assured her I was, now.

"Take the day off," she said. "Lee, you've worked ten straight days getting ready for WinterFest. Dolly and I can handle things. We're only open from eleven to five today."

So Joe and I lolled around the house all day. Joe built a fire in the fireplace. We got some steaks out of the freezer. We watched television. We even got out the videotape Gordon Hitchcock had brought by and looked at all the WinterFest coverage. Seeing five clips of Mozelle talking about the wonderful-ness of Warner Pier failed to cheer me up.

Then Joe flipped on the Grand Rapids news and Gordon Hitchcock appeared on the screen again, live and in color. My escapade at Warner Point was the third item on the news, right after an eight-car pile-up on East Beltline.

Gordon put on a small smile before he began his report. "Warner Pier chocolatier Lee Woodyard claims she was the object of a wild predawn chase by—get this, folks—a snowman. Warner Pier authorities say they are investigating links between this alleged crime and the Lake Michigan resort's annual Winter Festival, which this year is using a snowman as a logo."

"Oh, no!" Joe and I said it in unison.

Gordon went on. "Woodyard and her husband—Joe Woodyard is Warner Pier city attorney—are already being questioned by police in connection with two killings. . . ."

Blah, blah, blah. He quoted a "state police spokesman," but his primary source, obviously, was McCullough. Joe and I were figuratively tarred and feathered.

I was too angry to cry about it. "Jerk!" I said. I'm not sure if I meant McCullough or Gordon Hitchcock.

Hitchcock closed his report with film of me, part of the film his photographer had taken in the shop the day earlier. And he climaxed his story with the moment when I'd lost it.

There I was, facing the camera. "Mary Samson was as sweet, shy, and kind a person as anyone who ever lived. She was killed in a cruel way. I'm not going to sensationalize her death so you can increase your ratings. Please leave."

Then they showed what happened next. They showed the moment when tears welled up, and the moment when I turned and walked away.

Joe reached over and hugged me. "Not bad! You zinged that creep."

"What do you mean?"

"I mean that you came across as a regular human being and as a person intelligent enough to know how Gordon Hitchcock was trying to exploit you."

I hoped he was right. I hoped it hadn't looked like I was the one trying to exploit Mary's death.

The next morning Hogan and Joe came by the shop, and Aunt Nettie and I had coffee with them in our break room—I was still working back there—and chewed over the case.

Aunt Nettie was still sure that Mendenhall would have been looking for companionship after I dumped him. Paid companionship.

"The desk clerk absolutely denies that he called anybody for Mendenhall," Hogan said. "And neither Mendenhall's phone nor the motel phone records show any numbers that might have been for a call girl."

Aunt Nettie wasn't convinced. "Could Mendenhall have—well, gone looking for one?"

Hogan laughed. "Not without taking a cab, Nettie. That motel's in a newly developed suburban shopping center. Prostitutes don't stroll around in supermarkets, fast food joints, lumberyards, and everything-for-a-dollar stores."

"There aren't any bars?" She looked disappointed.

"Nope. There are no bars or taverns for a mile or more. There's a slightly more upscale motel a block away. They have a bar, but it's not the kind of place to cater to the vice scene."

"Poor Mendenhall," I said sarcastically. "Almost out of booze, and he couldn't even get a drink."

Hogan looked surprised. "Oh, Mendenhall had a full bottle, Lee. Or half full. It was sitting on the table in the crime scene photos."

"All I saw him with was that little flask. It wouldn't hold much to begin with, and when I dropped him off, it was nearly empty."

"How do you know?"

"It's in my statement for McCullough. Mendenhall handed it to me, tried to get me to have a drink with him." I shuddered. "The idea of touching my mouth to something that creep . . . Well, believe me, I didn't take a drink. But I held the flask in my hand, and I thought it was nearly empty. Maybe he had a bottle in his luggage."

"Surely not!" Aunt Nettie sounded shocked. "It's illegal to take alcoholic beverages onto a plane."

Hogan grinned. "It's been done, however. But I think Mendenhall probably just walked over to the supermarket and bought a bottle."

"Does anybody remember seeing him over there?"

"I don't know if McCullough asked about it. It didn't seem too important."

I guess that would have been the end of that, if I hadn't had to go to Grand Rapids that afternoon.

We got an unexpected call from a customer—a gift shop. They needed a fresh supply of Santa Claus figures. The UPS man had already gone when they called, and it was a large enough order that I agreed to drive it up. Maybe I only wanted a reason to get out of the shop for a while.

Aunt Nettie enthusiastically approved of my trip. That was the first surprise. The next surprise was that she decided to go along.

I blinked hard. "Go with me? Now?"

"Isn't that when you're going?"

"Yes, but you rarely leave the shop when we're so busy."

"I'm not indispensable. Dolly can handle things. I'll get my coat and help you load up the Santas."

We were on the road by three o'clock. I wondered if Aunt Nettie had something she wanted to discuss privately, but nothing came up. We made it to our customer's shop and were unloading by four. As we got back in the van, Aunt Nettie gave a happy smile.

"All right," she said. "Now we can do what I really wanted to do."

"What's that? A Christmas gift for Hogan?"

"Oh, no! I ordered him something in September."

"Then what is it?"

"I want to see that motel where Mendenhall was killed."

Chapter 16

"You minx!" I said. "You're as nosy as I am."

"Now, Lee, I just want to get an idea of the layout."

"There's nothing special about that motel. It's just like every other cheap chain motel. I didn't think Mendenhall needed to stay at the Ritz. It's the kind of motel that's not likely to be particular about its customers."

"I'm sure it is just that. But I'd like to see it."

I didn't argue anymore. I drove over there—a trip that required an extra thirty minutes of late-afternoon city traffic. I pulled in and stopped in the parking lot. "See. It's very ordinary."

"Where was Mendenhall's room?"

I drove around the building and pointed it out. "Room one twenty-two. Ground floor."

Aunt Nettie looked the surroundings over. "It's just before five o'clock, isn't it? Isn't that the time of day you dropped Mendenhall off?"

"I guess so."

"Maybe we should see if that same clerk is on duty."

"That creep!"

"You can wait in the van."

"Oh, no! I'm not too wimpy to face down a sleazy desk clerk."

We drove around the motel and parked near the motel's entrance. Through the window I saw that same desk clerk—the one who had offered to do me a favor if I did him one—at the desk. His hair looked slicker than ever. I groaned to myself, but I got out of the van and followed Aunt Nettie inside.

However, I didn't have to "face down" the clerk. Aunt Nettie simply approached him, smiled her sweetest smile, and picked up the name plate on the desk. It read GARY.

"Hello, Gary," Aunt Nettie said. "I'm Nettie Jones from Warner Pier. You probably remember my niece. Last week she accidentally got involved in that terrible situation when poor Professor Mendenhall was killed here."

Gary looked wary. "Yes. I remember her."

"She and I are trying to help with the investigation—you may know that my husband is police chief down at Warner Pier—and I'd appreciate your answering a few questions." She smiled sweetly again.

By now the clerk was ready to help this sweet old lady any way she wanted. He nodded.

That was when Aunt Nettie zinged him. "After Lee dumped that man off, leaving him disappointed, did he try to find other companionship? Professional companionship?"

Gary Smith blinked. Then he recoiled. "Well, Mrs. . . . I wouldn't . . ."

"Come now. I'm sure you're not personally involved in the vice scene. But motel patrons have been known to seek such services. That's no secret. And who else could Mendenhall ask for a local contact?"

"I told the police he didn't do that. Mendenhall did come by the desk. He was really steamed! Now I see . . . I guess he was mad because your niece dumped him. But all he asked was where he could get another bottle. That's the only time I saw him after he checked in. I didn't have any numbers for him to call, he didn't ask me for one, and I didn't give him any."

"So he didn't ask you where he could find a date?"

Gary's gaze shifted sideways. "I just work on the desk. I don't have anything going on the side."

Aunt Nettie's face fell. "I didn't mean to insult you. We're just so eager to trace everything Mendenhall did after Lee left him here."

"I told the cops the truth." The clerk sighed. "Listen, around here I'm just a peon. If you want to know what's really happening, you talk to Raymond."

"Raymond? Is he the manager?"

"He might as well be. I don't dare cross him because he could get me fired. But Raymond's job is night custodian." Gary leaned across the desk and lowered his voice. "Raymond Kirby is the only custodian I ever heard of who drives a Mercedes."

Aunt Nettie said, "Oh," but she meant, "Aha!"

Gary's face grew serious. "Don't let Raymond know I sent the cops after him. I can't afford to get crosswise with him."

That was all he was going to tell us. But it was something. Aunt Nettie's sweet face and little-old-lady act had pried some actual information out of him. It was information that Hogan, Sergeant McCullough, and Alex VanDam apparently had not learned: The night custodian handled the vice situation at Motel Sleaze. The desk clerk had been instructed to pass any inquiries from guests on to Raymond.

Aunt Nettie smiled proudly. "And where can we find Raymond?"

That's when I jumped in. "Oh, no, Aunt Nettie! Now we call Hogan!"

I was not prepared to beard Raymond in his toolshed, and

I wasn't going to let Aunt Nettie do it either. A night custodian who could intimidate young male desk clerks and who was prepared to provide prostitutes for patrons of a sleazy motel was not someone I wanted to talk to without large, tough, burly police people to back me up.

I was relieved when Gary said Raymond was on his dinner break and wouldn't be back for half an hour, "if then." This gave me a chance to convince Aunt Nettie it would be better to leave questioning Raymond to professionals.

I got her outside; then Aunt Nettie stopped to argue. "Lee, this Raymond might admit something to us that he wouldn't tell the detectives."

"But if we tip him off, the police won't be able to question him effectively. He might even run. Let's ask Hogan what to do."

Aunt Nettie finally agreed, but she insisted that we continue her plan to retrace Mendenhall's steps. Literally. We walked around the motel, sticking to the cleared sidewalks, the way Mendenhall would have. Then we slogged through the slush to cross that extremely busy street I remembered from my first stop there. We took the shortest route to reach the cleared sidewalks of a strip shopping center, a center that held an appliance store, a pet supply place, a beauty shop, a chain store selling discount shoes, and a Chinese takeout restaurant. Then we had to walk through another parking lot, filled with more slush, to reach the supermarket. Inside, we went to the liquor, wine, and beer section. We looked at the bourbon display. We walked back outside, retraced our steps past the shops in the adjoining mall—the giant-screen television sets in the appliance store window featured Gordon Hitchcock pontificating—and dared death by heavy traffic to get back to the motel.

I sighed with relief when I got Aunt Nettie buckled into the van. We had crossed an extremely busy street—twice—

without being flattened by some suburban mother trying to get the kids home from basketball practice. I thought the whole episode was pointless, but I didn't tell Aunt Nettie that. I simply offered her my cell phone so she could call Hogan and tell him what we'd found out from the desk clerk.

But that probably was pointless, too. Even if the detectives were able to prove Mendenhall entertained a prostitute in his room, it wouldn't explain what I considered the key mystery we had to solve to figure out who killed him. It would not explain how Mendenhall's cell phone wound up in the pocket of my coat. No Grand Rapids prostitute had put it there. It had been planted by someone from Warner Pier.

To McCullough, of course, there was no mystery about that. Either Joe or I had taken the phone from the scene to cover up our guilt in his death. To him the only mystery was why we had kept the phone, instead of tossing it in the river. Actually, he could probably answer that one, too: Rivers were covered with ice right at the moment.

Anyway, Aunt Nettie and I had looked over the situation at the motel, and she had dug a little information out of the desk clerk. We drove home, fighting commuter traffic in the winter dark. Apparently I looked pitiful when I got to the house, because Joe offered me dinner out. I requested Warner Point.

Joe looked surprised that I was willing to return to the place where I'd been chased by the sinister snowman thirty-six hours earlier. From my viewpoint, it was a case of getting back on the horse that threw me. Warner Point is a major center for Warner Pier activities, and I didn't want to get the heebie-jeebies about being chased by a snowman every time I had to enter that building. I determined that I'd go there every chance I got for the rest of the winter.

Aunt Nettie may have felt the same way. At least, we ran into her and Hogan there, and we joined them for dinner.

Aunt Nettie and I seemed to have trained Joe and Hogan

right; they didn't laugh at our afternoon of detective work. In fact, Hogan said he'd already passed along our information about Raymond Kirby to Sergeant McCullough and Alex VanDam.

"I hope you didn't tell them that it came from the desk clerk," I said. "He was scared stiff of that custodian guy."

Hogan grinned. "I told McCullough I got it from a reliable informant."

"He'll think one of your Warner Pier pals patronizes the place."

"Let him."

"But I don't really see what good all this will do. I'll never believe a call girl killed Mendenhall, not when his cell phone was found in my pocket thirty miles away, and I didn't put it there."

"You're right," Hogan said. "But if a call girl was there, she could be a witness."

The rest of the dinner conversation was more cheerful. We all made a conscious effort not to talk about the deaths of either Mendenhall or Mary Samson.

After we'd paid our bill and were saying good-bye to Jason, I noticed that the lights were on in the art exhibit rooms, across the hall from the restaurant.

I turned to Jason. "Is the art show still open?"

"Anytime the restaurant is open, the show is open."

"Joe, do you mind if we take another look? It was so crowded at the opening I missed a lot."

Joe didn't object. We waved Aunt Nettie and Hogan off, then went into the show for an nearly private view. I even picked up a catalog and took time to read it as we wandered through the show. Two other couples who had eaten at Warner Point came in, but we had the place almost to ourselves. It was a weeknight, and the Warner Pier Winter Arts Festival wouldn't draw a big crowd again until the weekend.

I guess the best part of a private showing is that you can make funny remarks about the art. I kept my voice down, because of the other couples, but I was able to tell Joe that I found Mozelle's watercolor so insipid that she must have used a bowl of milk toast for inspiration, that Johnny Owens' large metal statuary wasn't nearly as much fun as the little cartoons he drew at meetings and must have been a lot harder to display, and that another artist's bulbous purple nudes looked like the "before" pictures in diet drug ads. Joe had a few comments about something that looked like a warped cottage. The artist had experimented with perspective, but as a woodworker, Joe thought the building in the painting was going to fall down the first time a wind hit.

We both liked a modern painting that was all blocks of bright color. We were impressed by a tiny exquisite carving of three chickadees. And we both thought Bob VanWinkle-Snow's storm photo, the best-in-show winner, was stunning. Its price was stunning, too. We weren't tempted to buy it, even though thirty percent of the price would go to the WinterFest.

The catalog made an entertaining side note to all this. It started with a two-page synopsis explaining why the Warner Pier Arts Festival included a jurored art show. The rest of the booklet listed each artist, one per page. Each page had a reproduction of the art entered in the show, a short bio of the artist, and an artist's statement.

I learned that Bob VanWinkle-Snow had trained with some photographer I never heard of and that he strove for "realism filtered through creative vision." Johnny Owens had a degree in art from Waterford College, and he tried to bring out the "inner strength of the metal" he welded. I liked the work both of them did, but I merely thought their art was beautiful to look at.

"I'm just an accountant," I said to Joe. "I don't get these artist statements."

"They get pretty highfalutin," he said. "What does Mozelle have to say about her milk-toast watercolor?"

"I didn't notice." I thumbed through the book. Then I thumbed through it again. "She's not here."

"What? Mozelle missed a chance for some public notice?"

"It's out of character for Mozelle, isn't it? Besides Mary Samson helped put this little book together. I'm sure neither she nor George would skip an artist. But the artists are in alphabetical order. French should be here between Ervin and Garrity."

I looked at the booklet carefully. "Joe, Mozelle's page has been cut out."

"Surely not."

"Look!" I showed him where the page that would have held her name should have been. The page had been neatly sliced out. Only a eighth of an inch of the paper was left.

"Someone did that with a razor blade or a craft knife," Joe said. "How odd."

"Let's check to see if they're all that way."

We went back to the stack of twenty-five or so catalogs at the table by the entrance, and we checked all of them. Mozelle wasn't in there.

"Some other artist was on the back of her page," I said. "So there are two missing."

"There are probably more books someplace. I wonder if this page has been cut out of all of them."

"I think I have one of these at the office. Seems as if either Mary or George passed a few out at one of the meetings."

"Let's go over there and look. And speaking as a committee member, we'd better talk to George about this tomorrow. I hope this wasn't vandalism."

We went in the street door at TenHuis Chocolade, and I

went straight to the file drawer where I keep what I call my "club work." I don't really belong to clubs, but I do serve on a committee for the Warner Pier Chamber of Commerce, as well as the WinterFest committee, so I have papers that are not related to work. I try to keep them separate, and I was sure I'd stuck all the papers I picked up at WinterFest meetings in that drawer. The WinterFest financial records are on my office computer and are backed up on a CD.

It took a little digging, but I found the copy of the art show catalog that had been handed out early.

"Aha!" I waved it triumphantly. Joe leaned over my shoulder, and we looked for Mozelle.

"Here she is," I said, "right before Garrity. And on the other side is that artist Marie Fung."

We both read about Marie Fung. She lived in Chicago and produced art she adapted on the computer. I barely remembered her show entry. Joe nodded to indicate that he was finished with the page, so I flipped back to Mozelle's information. We both read it silently.

"Sounds pretty ordinary to me," Joe said. "She went to art school back east and then came home to join the Warner Pier art colony, not that the Warner Pier art colony noticed her presence."

"She attended Gerhard College."

"I never heard of it."

"Seems as if I have. But I don't know where."

As I gathered up my WinterFest papers to put them back in their drawer, I was completely mystified about Mozelle's biography and artist's statement being cut out of the art show catalog. Or had it been Marie Fung, the artist on the back of her page, who had been cut out?

Who on earth had done that? It had been a neat job that had been done carefully. It wasn't as if someone had ripped out a page to wrap up a wad of chewing gum.

Had all the catalogs been defaced in that way? Or only the ones out at the show? I vowed to check. When I got time. It was still Christmas season at TenHuis Chocolade. And I was a suspect in a murder case. Missing pages in an art show catalog would have to wait.

Chapter 17

Our late dinner, followed by a visit to the art show and a quick stop for a little detection, meant it was nearly eleven when we got home and got ready for bed. Suddenly I gave a gasp. "Oh gosh, Joe! This darn committee meets tomorrow."

"It does?"

"Eleven thirty at Warner Point. Dutch lunch. I'd completely forgotten that."

Joe sighed. "Seems as if once the whole thing is under way, it could run on its own. But it will be a good chance to ask George about the missing page from the catalog."

"Rats! I'll have to do a financial report first thing in the morning."

As I climbed into bed, I turned to Joe. "I guess Mozelle simply can't be the murderer."

"She's got a real good alibi."

"I know. But it's got to be someone from Warner Pier—because of where we found Mendenhall's telephone."

"Your pocket."

"Right. If the killer has to be someone I know, sending Mozelle up the river would bother me less than sending someone I like. My grandmother would say I'm completely lacking in Christian charity when it comes to Mozelle."

"I don't like her either. I wouldn't mind sending her up—as long as she was actually guilty. How about the snowman with the snow shovel? Could Mozelle have taken that role?"

I thought about it. "I suppose she might have. I think we can deduce that the snowman's head was not worn by anyone who was in tiptop condition. If the person had been stronger or had more stamina, he or she would have caught me." I shuddered, and Joe pulled me over close to him so that when I went on talking, I was speaking into his neck. "That crazy head—thanks to it I can't guess at the snowman's height, and it sure hid the person's face."

"So it could have been Mozelle," Joe said. "Of course, if we're making a list of people who might have killed Mendenhall, Mozelle is not really a possibility."

"I know. She was in Chicago. At a very fancy hotel."

"Yep. Besides, her phone number was not on that list George Jenkins sent to Mendenhall. She wouldn't have known where Mendenhall was, and he wouldn't have known how to find her. If he'd had any reason to."

We dropped the discussion then, and after a while we went to sleep.

At the breakfast table, I dragged out my list of committee members and their alibis for the night Mendenhall died.

Maggie McNutt had been at play practice. George Jenkins and Ramona had been together, hashing out a problem about the art show, until seven. After that, Ramona had been at home with her husband, and George had made a trip to Wal-Mart. Sarajane had also gone to Wal-Mart that evening. That wasn't as coincidental as it might seem. Warner Pier doesn't have a Wal-Mart, but it's impossible to enter either the one in Holland or the one in South Haven without running into a fellow Pier-ite.

Amos Hart had been rehearsing the WinterFest Chorus, so he had about fifty people to back up his whereabouts. Both

Jason and Johnny Owens claimed to have been home—Jason going to bed early, but with his partner and his partner's grown son in the house, and Johnny watching a DVD of a Disney film when he wasn't talking to an art dealer who called from Chicago.

I didn't try to count the people who might have answered committee members' telephones, people like Ramona's husband, Bob VanWinkle-Snow. Bob had admitted he once had a public argument with Mendenhall, and I hadn't found out if he had an alibi for the night the guy died.

But I didn't want any of these people to be guilty. I wanted Mozelle to be guilty. And that didn't look likely.

At least I was going to see the rest of the WinterFest committee the next day, so I could check on how many more catalogs were floating around. Then we could find out if Mozelle and Marie Fung had been clipped out of all of them.

My head was spinning at eleven fifteen the next morning, when I drove onto the grounds of Warner Point for the WinterFest committee meeting. It seemed as if the situation couldn't get any more confused.

At least that was what I thought until I saw Gordon Hitchcock and his photographer in the circular drive in front of the building, getting equipment out of an LMTV van.

I rushed inside, eager to avoid another interview, and immediately ran into Chuck O'Riley, editor of the *Warner Pier Gazette*. He was sitting in the dining room, near a long table Jason had apparently set up for our meeting.

"Yikes!" I said. "LMTV is outside, and you're inside. Is there going to be a news conference?"

Chuck looked slightly pained. "The WinterFest committee is big news all of a sudden. When two people connected with the committee get murdered, it has that effect."

Ramona was already in her place at the head of the meeting table. She switched her long gray ponytail around as if it were a real pony's tail and glared at Chuck. "Not a thing is going to go on at this meeting but routine business. We have nothing to do with a crime investigation. It's just a progress report."

I shrugged. "I can snow 'em with really boring financials. We'll have the reporters sound asleep in five minutes."

That drew only a small smile from Ramona. "I've been swamped with press calls since Mary died," she said. "The reporters have been much more annoying than the police."

Joe's voice came from the door. "That's because the police think they know who did it."

He took me by the arm and led me over to Ramona. He took her arm with his other hand and marched the two of us into a corner, well away from Chuck O'Riley. When he spoke, his voice was low, but firm.

"Ramona, I'm sure you understand that the cops—at least the Lake Knapp cops—consider Lee and me the main suspects."

"That's ridiculous!" Bless Ramona's heart. She sounded outraged.

Joe spoke again, still keeping his voice low. "I appreciate your support. But that's the situation right now. Would it be best for the committee if Lee and I both resigned?"

Ramona stared at him for a long moment. Then she spoke. "No!"

"It might take the heat off you."

Ramona drew herself up, switched her ponytail again, and spoke loudly. "If I can't stand some heat, I'd better get off the committee. We can't do without you and Lee."

Then she turned and went back to the head of the table just as Gordon Hitchcock and his cameraman came in.

"Welcome," she said firmly. "Thanks for coming. The WinterFest committee was formed to publicize Warner Pier and bring business to our community. We're delighted that a Grand Rapids news medium is covering our activities."

"Actually, we're here to ask questions," Gordon Hitch-cock said.

Ramona looked at her watch. "Then ask quickly. We're all businesspeople. That's why we're meeting over lunch."

Gordon signaled, and his cameraman began to film.

"Two people connected with the Warner Pier WinterFest have been murdered. Are you continuing with the scheduled activities?"

"Of course." Ramona's voice was firm. "I've discussed this with the investigating officers, and they see no point in canceling our plans."

"Does that seem—well—heartless?"

"We are all grieving for Mary Samson, who was a long-time member of our community and a friend to most of us. Of course, none of us knew Professor Mendenhall, so his death is not such a personal loss. However, the Warner Pier WinterFest has never pretended to be anything other than what it is—a business promotion for our town."

"But—" Gordon Hitchcock tried to say something, and Ramona stopped him with a gesture. She kept on talking.

"Our business community has sunk a lot of money into preparing and promoting this year's WinterFest. We would be failing our responsibilities if we simply dropped the whole thing because of these unfortunate occurrences."

"But what about danger to people who come to the WinterFest?"

"There is no danger to WinterFest patrons. I've talked about this with our local police chief and with Lieutenant VanDam of the Michigan State Police. Neither of them feels that there's any threat at all to people who come to our art show, who attend our musical and dramatic performances, who visit our terrific shops and art galleries, or who eat in our delightful restaurants. The danger is that they'll stay home and miss the fun."

"Do you have any idea who might have killed Professor Mendenhall or Ms. Samson?"

"No. And if I did, I wouldn't tell you and your camera. I'd pass that information along to the proper authorities."

Gordon and the cameraman stopped filming. They took seats near Chuck, where they drew curious gazes as the other committee members came in. George Jenkins looked more tweedy than ever, Amos Hart wore his bow tie and snow boots, Johnny Owen carried his doodling pad and pencil, and Sarajane wore a woodsman outfit of wool plaid shirt and jeans.

Jason pulled up a small table for the press so they could eat, too. Only two committee members were not present by the time we had all ordered our food, and Ramona called the meeting to order. Maggie McNutt and Mozelle were not there.

Maggie had a conflict with her duties as a teacher at Warner Pier High School, Ramona announced, and had phoned in a report that morning. But there was no explanation as to why Mozelle wasn't there. Her absence seemed odd, because Mozelle was always there and always early.

Sarajane passed out the minutes, giving copies to Gordon Hitchcock and to Chuck. We approved them. Then Ramona called for the financial report.

The report had taken me an hour I didn't have to spare, but I had it ready. I passed copies around the table and handed copies to Gordon Hitchcock and Chuck O'Riley. I read off the highlights.

Then I heard a voice from the press section. Gordon Hitchcock was on his feet. "May I ask a question?"

"Certainly," Ramona said. "Although our committee, as a private organization, is not covered by the Michigan open-meeting law, our proceedings are completely public."

"Ms. Woodyard, I see by your financial report that the

play, for example, is going to cost twice as much to produce as it is projected to bring in."

"That's correct."

"Then how can the festival make any money?"

"The festival doesn't intend to make money on individual events, Mr. Hitchcock. The events are planned to draw people to Warner Pier. We hope they'll eat dinner, shop, maybe stay overnight in our of our bed-and-breakfast inns. We hope the events will break even. Any money the events make above their expenses is gravy. Seed money for next year."

"Yes," Ramona said. "The concerts, the play, the art show—those are gifts to the public. That's why we keep the tickets cheap. Our merchants donate money for those. They hope to make it up, as Lee said, in meals, shopping, overnight stays."

"Oh." Gordon Hitchcock sat down. He looked puzzled.

I leaned toward him. "Talk to your ad director," I said. "It's similar to what Wal-Mart calls a 'loss leader.' The point is to get the people into the stores."

I guess my report really did make the news media need a nap. Anyway, I'd hardly finished when Gordon and his cameraman got up and left. Chuck followed them out.

"They missed the chocolates," I said. "I forgot to put them out before the meeting. I brought snowmen this time."

"It's better to have them after lunch, anyway," Ramona said. "I don't mind not offering to share with the LMTV crew."

Amos Hart drew a breath that practically took all the oxygen out of the room. "Now that they're gone—perhaps we don't have to try so hard to present a united front."

Ramona's tone was brisk. "Actually, Amos, we don't have to present a united front at any time. Is your item a committee report or should it come under new business?"

Amos seemed to sag as he exhaled. It seemed he didn't like to be reminded that Ramona ran our meetings according to Robert's Rules of Order. He said he'd wait for his report. He took a milk chocolate snowman and laid it beside his water glass. And just then the waitress brought our meals in, and action stopped while we were all served. Jason brought in a sandwich for himself and sat down with us.

The meeting went on as soon as we all had butter and salt and pepper, but as we chewed, all of us had plenty of time to get curious before Ramona called on Amos for his report.

He inhaled again. "I hate to sound like a martyr," he said, "but I really feel that the choral activities of this year's WinterFest are being slighted."

"But your chorus doesn't sing until next weekend, Amos." Ramona sounded patient.

"Yes! That means there should be publicity in the Grand Rapids papers and on the television stations this week."

"I know. Losing Mary really messed the publicity up. I'm not sure what she'd turned in and what she hadn't. And I'm not sure how to find out."

"Chuck might be able to help you," Joe said. "She probably sent all the news releases out at the same time, and he ought to know if the *Gazette* received one."

The discussion went on as discussions do—pointless and nitpicky. Amos began moaning about extraneous subjects. He driveled on because he didn't want to have to drive to Grand Rapids for something or other, because the last time he'd driven up there he'd gotten caught in a snowstorm, but if the stoles for the choir—the ones in bright, holiday colors—didn't come in, he'd have to go, and the WinterFest committee ought to pay for his gas, and even though more people took part in the chorus than in any other WinterFest activity, all the committee did was talk about the art show. And why make the effort to get the stoles? Because if no news media paid attention to the chorus, no one would come to their performances anyway.

It was so annoying I could have pulled my hair out by handfuls. I tried to think about something else. Like the snowman. Listening to Amos drivel on reminded me that he'd said he had seen them before they were revealed to the public. I still wondered where. He kept talking. After eight minutes, I spoke up. "Listen, Amos. I know Mary had all the news releases roughed out before the WinterFest even started. I'll bet I can find them in her computer and—"

Joe interrupted. "Her computer is still part of a crime scene, Lee."

"Drat!"

There was a moment of silence; then Joe spoke again. "I'll talk to Hogan and Alex VanDam. Maybe they'll let you into Mary's house to look at her computer, Lee."

"It's worth a try."

"She's probably got a list of fax numbers for the news media, too," Joe said, "or their e-mails. Mary had contacts in Grand Rapids, Chicago, and Detroit, all over the area. She must have had a master list. Lee and I can try to piece it together this evening and get the last-minute releases off by tomorrow."

Amos looked mollified for a moment. Then he looked astonished. He was staring at something behind us, and Joe and I both whipped our heads around to see what it was.

A woman was charging into the dining room, headed for our table. For a moment I didn't recognize her. Then I realized it was Mozelle. She was not her usual calm, contained self.

Her sleek chignon was not sleek. It was messy. There was a smudge on her nose. She was wearing a puffy down coat, which was askew. Her expression was deranged.

"There you are!" Her voice was almost a scream. "One of you must know! Why was my page cut out of the art show catalog?"

Really Sinful Chocolate

Chocolate may have actually been "devil's food" for one famed lover of the stuff—the fabled Marquis de Sade.

De Sade, who inspired the word "sadism," was born into an aristocratic French family in 1740. He had a long and strange life, with thirty years of it spent in madhouses. However, in the authoritative book *A True History of Chocolate* authors Sophie D. and Michael D. Coe report that he may have been accused of atrocities he merely imagined for his "inflammatory, deeply subversive fiction." Whatever the true story, de Sade was jailed by the French government both before and after the revolution. When he fled France, he was jailed in Sardinia.

Through it all, de Sade loved sweets, particularly chocolate. He frequently asked his long-suffering wife, who never deserted him, to send packages to him in prison or in a madhouse. He requested chocolate candy, chocolate cakes, chocolate bars, chocolate for drinking, and even chocolate suppositories, then a remedy for piles.

Chapter 18

I could feel my jaw drop clear to my breastbone, and everyone else at the table was gaping just as widely. To Mozelle we must have looked like a stringer of Lake Michigan whitefish flopping in the bottom of a boat.

It wasn't the news that her page had been cut out of the catalog that was making me gape. After all, I knew that. The surprise was Mozelle herself. I had had no idea that she could lose her cool in public like that, and I don't think the rest of the committee did either.

Mozelle hadn't found her cool either. She kept talking, and her voice was strident. "I find it hard to believe that anyone would stoop so low! I know everyone on this committee hates me, but I never thought anyone would actually do me deliberate harm."

Ramona spoke calmly. "Mozelle, what are you talking about?"

Mozelle brandished an art show catalog as if it were a revolutionary pamphlet. "I'm talking about this! Your precious husband is in it! Johnny is in it! Every other entry in the show is in it. But my page has been sliced out!"

She tossed the booklet down on the table, where it knocked over a small container of mayonnaise. Then she folded her arms and glared at us all in an attitude that combined defiance and fury.

Ramona picked up the catalog and examined it. "You're right, Mozelle. The page has been deliberately sliced out of this one. But surely they're not all like that."

"They are! I've checked. All the ones on the table as you go into the show are like that. And all the ones in the storage room. Every single one!"

"All of them?" That was George. His voice was awed. "All five hundred? All defaced?"

"I suppose some were taken away last weekend," Mozelle said. "I can't check on those."

Ramona looked up, frowning. "Lee, can we afford to get the catalog reprinted?"

"It would be expensive." I looked through my papers, searching for the invoice from the printer. "I know the original cost was several thousand dollars. Mozelle, do you think we could print an insert? If we put an extra sheet in each copy, it might not be as good as having the page in its proper place. But that would be better than having you and Marie Fong not in at all."

Mozelle looked at me accusingly. "And just how did you know Marie Fong was on the back of the page?"

"Because Joe and I went through the show last night, and we picked up a catalog, and we noticed then that the page with you on one side and Ms. Fong on the other had been cut out of the dozen or so booklets there by the door. I was going to ask George about it today. I thought—well, it had been done so neatly I thought there might have been some reason for cutting the page out."

"Oh, no," George said. "I don't know anything about it. This is terrible."

Ramona spoke to me. "Could the printer do an insert?"

"I'm sure he could. TenHuis Chocolade deals with this

same printer—we think they do the best color work in our area, and they're competitive on price. They keep our sales material in their computer, and when we need a thousand more brochures, we call, and they print them out. I'd have to check, of course, but I imagine they'd still have the whole art show catalog available. It shouldn't be any trick to print out those two pages."

I turned to Mozelle. "We might have to pay a premium to get it done by the weekend, but I think we can find the money."

Mozelle didn't look mollified. "If—if the printer still has the pages in his computer files."

I tried to sound confident. "I still have one of the catalogs George and Mary handed out as samples. That page is still in it. If the printer doesn't have the original files, the type could be reset from that. And I'm sure George still has the original slides used to scan the artwork."

George nodded. "Oh, yes, I have the slides. I'm sure we can get an insert printed."

Mozelle deflated into a chair, but she was sitting up straight. She seemed calmer, more like her authoritative self. "It would be quite an expense."

"It must be done!" George's voice was firm. "Mozelle, we want this to be a respected art show, one artists try hard to get in. We can't expect top artists to enter if they're not treated properly. If a mistake is made, we have to fix it."

A murmur of agreement went around the table. Jason, ever the restaurateur, jumped to his feet and offered to get Mozelle some lunch. Amos Hart patted her shoulder, though that didn't seem to comfort Mozelle. Johnny Owens examined the catalog she'd tossed onto the table and muttered a few opinions about the ancestry of anybody who would do such a thing to an artist. Joe got up from the table and asked Jason if he could use the telephone. He received permission and left the room.

Mozelle seemed genuinely appreciative of everyone's concern. "Thank you. All of you. I apologize for losing my temper."

We all assured her that we understood her feelings, and the board quickly voted to fund the extra printing as a non-budget item.

In the lull that followed the vote, I spoke. "Now we call the police."

Joe was back. "I called them after George made it clear he knew of no reason for the page to be cut out of the catalog."

Ramona looked surprised. "Do we have to involve the police?"

I spoke before Joe could. "Of course! Ramona, this was vandalism. Or malicious mischief. It's going to cost the committee quite a lot money to rectify the situation. It was a crime!"

"But it's such bad publicity," Ramona said.

"I'm sorry about that. But we can't simply ignore it." I'm sure I sounded miffed. I was the one who was going to have to find the money.

Joe did his lawyer thing at that point, clearing his throat in a way that made all eyes turn toward him. "We need to figure out who the heck cut that page out of the catalog, and why the heck they did it. And it's not only because we can't ignore vandalism. It's a lot more important than that."

He had everybody's attention. "Several strange things have happened in the past few days, and they all seem to center on this committee."

Ramona frowned. "What do you mean?"

"I mean two killings and an attempt on Lee's life. And now this."

A mutter of objections broke out, but Joe spoke again and quelled the opposition. "Let's face facts. First, Mendenhall, the juror for our art show, is killed. Of course, we all hoped it was nothing to do with us. We hoped he was killed because he was an obnoxious drunk who took up with the wrong drinking buddy. Or something."

"Wasn't that the reason?" Sarajane asked the question.

"I thought it might be to begin with, but Mary Samson's death put an end to that theory."

Sarajane wasn't convinced. "Mary was killed when she surprised a burglar!"

"Mary was the only member of the committee who admitted talking to Mendenhall. We can't ignore that link."

It was my turn to object. "But Mary said Mendenhall didn't say anything intelligent. She thought he was just a crank caller. She hung up on him."

"There's got to be a connection, Lee. It's too coincidental. First Mendenhall, then Mary. Then, after Mary was killed, someone lured you out here to Warner Point before daybreak and tried to brain you with a snow shovel." He patted my hand. "God knows why. I sure don't, and you don't seem to know either."

Then he turned back to the rest of the committee. "And now we have a case of vandalism. That's not as serious as murder, true. But we can't just assume that this committee is the target of a weird crime spree for no reason. There's something that links all these things."

Everyone at the table was staring at him as he went on. "The police will not be able to find the link unless each one of us gives them all the help we can. I think—and I believe Chief Jones agrees with me—that the whole series of events must key on Mendenhall. But Mendenhall appears"—he repeated the word—"*appears* to have been a complete stranger to Warner Pier and to everyone on the committee."

He paused while that sank in. "If that's not true, the detectives need to know it. If any of you knew Mendenhall before he came here, the police need to know. No matter how innocent your contact with him was."

Ramona frowned. "Bob and I had run into him at art shows. He and Bob had a blowup once. We already told the police about that."

"And I had a couple of classes with him at Waterford," Johnny Owens said. "I told the cops about that, too."

"That's the kind of thing I mean," Joe said. "If any of you ever had any connection with Mendenhall—or if any of you knows of someone who did—tell Hogan. No matter how minor it was."

He paused for dramatic effect. "It might save your life."

We heard a siren outside. Hogan was there.

Joe spoke one more time, raising his voice over the noise. "I'd advise you to hang around until we see if Hogan wants to talk to each of us individually."

George and Joe met Hogan at the front door and took him into the inner recesses of Warner Point to show him the defaced catalogs. The rest of us concluded the meeting. Nobody had much to say. After Joe's speech, our actions were anticlimactic.

As soon as the meeting adjourned I got on Jason's phone and called the printer. After I told him what had happened, he agreed to do a hurry-up job on an insert for the catalog.

I turned to Mozelle. "The printer still has the original pages in his computer. He says he'll run off inserts tonight. We can pick them up tomorrow morning."

She shook her head. "I feel very foolish about the fit I threw over this."

"Forget it." I was feeling uncomfortable. Her rant, including the accusation that "everyone on this committee hates me," was a bit too close to the truth, at least the truth of how I felt about her. I wanted to change the subject. So I asked a question. "Mozelle, your bio said you went to Gerhard College?"

"Yes. For two years."

"Where is that?"

"It's in Maryland. They had a top-notch art department, small but good. It was a girls' school." She shrugged. "They still had girls' schools in my day."

"It seems as if I've run into a mention of Gerhard College recently. But I can't remember where."

"I can't imagine anybody but alumnae mentioning it. It closed up years ago."

Amos Hart jumped into the conversation then with an abrupt question. "Lee, you were the only person to have any contact with Mendenhall. Did he say anything about knowing anybody in west Michigan?"

"He told me this was his first visit to Michigan. And he didn't indicate he knew anybody. Of course, he had met Ramona and Bob, and he might have remembered Johnny, since he was a former student. But he didn't mention having friends or acquaintances in the area."

Amos put a proprietary hand on Mozelle's shoulder. "I just hate for this sweet little lady to be bothered—and, yes, persecuted—over this mess when I know she didn't have anything to do with it."

Sweet little lady? That wasn't exactly the description I would have used to describe Mozelle. I bit my tongue.

But Mozelle didn't bite hers. She shook Amos' hand off, and she popped to her feet like a jack-in-the-box whose lid had just been lifted. "Amos," she said, "let's talk for a minute."

He followed meekly as she led him out into the restaurant's entrance hall.

I guess she thought they were out of earshot. She was wrong. I could hear their conversation plainly, even though I ducked my head and studied my financial report for all it was worth.

"Amos," Mozelle said, "please do not put your hand on me again."

"Mozelle! I didn't mean to offend you."

"I'm sure you didn't. But it's giving people the wrong impression."

"The wrong impression?"

"Yes. Just because we attended one or two events together, we are not a permanent couple."

"But I'd like for us to become a permanent couple, Mozelle."

"I'm sorry, Amos. I'm afraid I value my independence. I enjoy your companionship, of course. But that's all I'm interested in. If you want a more permanent relationship, I'm afraid you'll have to look elsewhere. And in the future please do not refer to me as a 'sweet little lady.' "

Frantically, I began to scribble on my report, trying to seem busy. I was afraid to get up; if my chair made a sound, Mozelle and Amos might figure out I'd overheard them. I didn't look up when Mozelle came back inside the restaurant. She sat down beside me, her lips in a tight line. Amos did not follow her in.

I was still trying to look occupied, and now I remembered I'd meant to take another look at Mendenhall's résumé. I dug through my folders until I found the copy that George Jenkins had passed around at the meeting when he told us about acquiring a new juror.

I looked the résumé over, trying to give the impression that it required all my concentration. I was curious about it, true, but my main intent was to distract Mozelle so that she wouldn't know I'd overheard her as she gave Amos the push.

Not that I blamed her for dumping him. The "sweet little lady" bit had been a step too far.

Still trying to look as if my mind were fully occupied with subjects that had nothing to do with Mozelle, I ran my finger down the résumé. It was the old-fashioned, detailed kind. It listed every show Mendenhall had jurored, every class he had taught, every award he had won. And I admit he had won a few. When I reached the final page—"Professional History"— one item caught my eye. My heart had just begun to pound when I heard Hogan's voice.

He was apparently addressing the entire room. "Thanks for staying. I think that for now we can just ask general questions. Does anyone have any idea how the catalogs came to be damaged?"

No one spoke.

Hogan nodded. "You can go. I may be calling you."

We all began to gather up our belongings. I stuffed Mendenhall's résumé back into my folder. "Hogan," I said, "I need to talk to you a minute."

"Can it wait?"

"Not very well." I tried to keep the excitement out of my voice.

He sighed deeply. "What is it?"

Enlightened by Mozelle's faux pas—talking to Amos without realizing I could hear ever word she said—I led him clear across the room, to a spot next to the French doors that led to the terrace. Then I pulled out Mendenhall's résumé.

"Look at this." I pointed to the "Professional History" section. "Look where Mendenhall was teaching thirty years ago."

"Gerhard College? Silvertown, Maryland? So?"

"That's where Mozelle studied art, Hogan! And he taught there as adjunct faculty for ten years. She must have known him."

Chapter 19

Hogan looked at the page. Then he shrugged. "So what?"

Talk about feeling let down. I nearly melted into my boots. But I plugged on. "You're wanting to know all about everyone who might have known Mendenhall. This proves that Mozelle did. Has she volunteered this information?"

"No, and I'll ask her about it, Lee. But it doesn't 'prove' anything, except that she might have known Mendenhall. And even if she did know him, it doesn't matter. She can't have killed him. She has an alibi."

"Oh, I know! She was in Chicago."

"Right. And Mendenhall didn't have her phone number. She's the only person on the WinterFest committee whose number is not in his cell phone. Plus, we've been assuming that whoever killed Mendenhall also killed Mary Samson. And Amos Hart says Mozelle was with him that evening."

Hogan again assured me that he'd ask Mozelle directly about any connection she'd ever had with Mendenhall, but I walked away with my tail feathers dragging.

Like Joe, I didn't believe in coincidences. Mozelle had studied art in a "small, but good" department, and Mendenhall had been teaching in that department at the same time. They simply must have known each other. How could I find out more?

I'd ask Aunt Nettie.

Aunt Nettie had lived in Warner Pier all her life, and she was a friendly soul who knew everybody and heard everything. Maybe the best thing about Aunt Nettie, however, was that she didn't tell everything she knew. As her niece, I appreciated that. During the time Joe and I were an item of Warner Pier gossip, and I was living with Aunt Nettie, we knew we could count on her not to discuss our personal affairs.

Aunt Nettie probably knew all about Mozelle, but getting her to tell what she knew might be a challenge.

When I came in the back door of TenHuis Chocolade, Aunt Nettie was sitting in the break room having a late lunch. I draped my coat over the back of a chair and sat down beside her. I decided on a direct approach.

"OK," I said. "Get ready for the third degree."

"What about?"

"Mozelle French. Anything you know about her."

"I don't know Mozelle very well. I knew her mother better. She died ten years ago."

"So Mozelle is a native of Warner Pier?"

"Oh, yes. Her father's father had a dry goods store on Peach Street back when it was a dirt road. You can see it in historic pictures. Smith's Mercantile."

"Smith. Was that Mozelle's maiden name?"

"Yes. Her mother was not from Warner Pier. She was from someplace in eastern Michigan." Aunt Nettie smiled. "Anna Smith wanted to be the grande dame of Warner Pier."

"The way Mozelle is today?"

"Something like that. But women's clubs and activities had more significance in those days. You girls today—you get your satisfaction out of your jobs. Or I hope you do, because you all seem to work so hard. But Anna Smith—in a town like Warner Pier, the only outlet her generation had was clubs, organizations, and tea parties. Being a club and social leader counted."

"Has Mozelle ever had a job?"

"Not that I know of. She was young when she married, and she plunged right into community organizations."

"She went to college."

"Yes, but that had more to do with social status than with learning a profession, at least as far as Mozelle's mother intended. Anna was old-fashioned in her outlook, didn't think women needed to worry about education. But she did recognize that if she wanted to see her daughter marry an educated man, she'd better have an educated daughter."

"Mozelle has a good mind and a tremendous amount of organizational ability. She could have had a successful career in business."

"Anna Smith wouldn't have approved. She never let Mozelle off the leash when she was young."

"It's hard to picture Mozelle on a leash." I laughed. "That's the kind of girl who goes wild when she gets away from home."

"Maybe that's why her mother only let her go away a couple of years."

Aunt Nettie clamped her lips together tightly. I began to feel that she knew more than she was telling.

"Come on, Aunt Nettie. Let me know the gossip about Mozelle. It might be important."

"Lee, anything I've ever heard was speculation. I'm not going to repeat it."

"What caused the speculation?"

"Warner Pier doesn't require a reason for speculation."

"I know that. And I appreciate you because you don't usually speculate. But something must have happened to Mozelle sometime in her life that caused some talk."

"It was so minor. An example of how the gossip mill works."

"I won't pass it around casually. What happened?"

"It was stupid. I mean, as a cause of gossip." Aunt Nettie sighed and gave in. "Mozelle left college in the middle of a semester."

I waited for the rest of the story. Then I realized that was all of it.

"That was it? Warner Pier gossiped about that?"

"Yes. Isn't it silly? Anna Smith said Mozelle had almost had pneumonia, and that she had come home to recover her health. But she didn't seem sick when she got home, and she never went back to college. The next year Mozelle married John French, and she's been here ever since, following in her mother's footsteps."

Aunt Nettie patted my hand. "So I can't tell you a single scandalous thing about Mozelle. She's just a bossy woman who likes to be a big frog in a small pond."

Our interview was over. My attempt to question Aunt Nettie had been a fiasco.

Time to try something else. I went to my computer and Googled Mozelle. All I found out was that she was in the newspapers a lot as a spokesman for the Warner Pier WinterFest and as president of this or that west Michigan activity.

I was still convinced that Mozelle must have at least known Dr. Fletcher Mendenhall when she attended Gerhard College. If their association was innocent—or even nonexistent—why hadn't she mentioned it? When Mendenhall's name first came up, wouldn't the natural thing have been for her to say, "Is that the one who taught at Gerhard College? He left the semester before I enrolled." Something.

Maybe, I decided, I could approach the question from a different angle. Johnny Owens had known Mendenhall in later years, at Waterford College, but he'd hinted that he'd heard some scandalous story about Mendenhall's earlier days. I could ask Johnny if he knew any more.

I referred to my list of WinterFest phone numbers and called Johnny. He answered on the second ring.

"Sorry to bother you, Johnny. Can you talk?"

"Sure. It'll help me put off a decision about the scale of this new piece."

"I wanted to know more about Mendenhall. You told us about the portrait of the trustee's wife with the birthmark. Was he involved in any other commotion when you knew him?"

"I think he'd learned to watch his step by then."

"By then?" I decided to make a wild and, as far as proof went, unfounded statement. "Do you mean after his problems at Gerhard College?"

"Yeah. But I don't know anything about that. Not really."

I almost clicked my heels. My unfounded statement had paid off. There had been a scandal when Mendenhall was at Gerhard.

Johnny was still talking. "Gerhard closed during my freshman year. About fifty of the girls transferred to Waterford. After they found out Mendenhall was there, they told the art students about him and his harem. That had been five or ten years earlier, and I don't think any of them had direct knowledge. So anything I know is a second- or thirdhand report."

"Just what were those thirdhand reports?"

"Well . . ."

"Johnny, I guessed that Mendenhall had some problems. I'd just like a few details. I promise to believe only half of what you tell me."

Johnny laughed. "The story was that some undergrad girl had moved in with Mendenhall. Her mother showed up and raised a stink."

"If the girl was living there willingly . . ."

"She may have been, but her mother threatened to sue the college. Mendenhall didn't have tenure, so he was fired."

I thought that over. "If he'd pressured the girl . . ."

"I don't really know any more, Lee. In fact, I don't know that much for sure." He paused. "I guess I can tell you the rest of the gossip. Supposedly another girl was living there, too."

"A ménage à trois?"

"A funhouse for Mendenhall. And I repeat, this story may be completely unfounded." Johnny chuckled. "Though the people who told about the situation had a nickname for the students involved. The flower girls. It seemed both of them were named for flowers. Rose and Lily. Something like that."

My heart sank. Let down again. Johnny's gossip had made me sure Mozelle, at age nineteen or so, had been involved with Mendenhall. That would explain her refusal, thirty or more years later, to admit she had known him. And the description of the mother who raised such a stink that Mendenhall was fired—well, that was exactly how a small-town "grande dame" would work.

But the "flower girl" name let Mozelle out. "Mozelle" was the name of a river and also of a wine. But as far as I'd ever heard, it was not the name of a flower. I thanked Johnny, then got out my dictionary and looked up the word "Mozelle" to make sure I was right. There was no mention of a flower by that name, but I learned that the river and the wine were spelled with an "s," not a "z."

As Aunt Nettie walked by I said as much. "Did you know Mozelle's mother couldn't spell? The French river is spelled M-o-s-e-l-l-e, not M-o-z-e-l-l-e, the way Mozelle spells it."

"It would have been her great-grandmother who couldn't spell. Mozelle was named for her two grandmothers."

"What's her other name?"

"Marguerite. Marguerite Mozelle Smith."

"She must have been in the third grade before she could spell all that."

Let down again. Unless . . . I grabbed the dictionary.

"Marguerite," it said, "same as a daisy (sense one)." I looked up daisy (sense one). That definition referred to the flower. It seemed Marguerite was either another name for a daisy or was a different type of daisy. Maybe both.

Aha!

Daisy might be a nickname for Marguerite. I could see a small-town girl going away to a "back east" college and wanting to use the more cosmopolitan Marguerite, rather than her Victorian-sounding, and misspelled, middle name. And from Marguerite to Daisy wouldn't be a long step, if they both referred to the same flower.

So it was possible that Mozelle had been one of the "flower girls."

I got so excited I called Hogan again. He didn't sound happy to hear my voice.

I asked him a question anyway. "Have you checked and double-checked Mozelle's Chicago alibi?"

Hogan groaned.

I told him the results of my research—if you can call two gossip sessions and looking up a couple of words in the dictionary research.

"I'll look into it," Hogan said. "But even if it's true, Mendenhall still did not have Mozelle's phone number. In fact, he probably didn't know her married name. And she was with Amos Hart when Mary Samson was killed."

"Amos would say anything for Mozelle, Hogan. I still think her Chicago alibi is worth checking out."

"Maybe. Lee, don't you have some work you need to get done?"

Hogan was right, of course. I buckled down for an hour, ordering special Amareena cherries to be used in Valentine bonbons and filling out the paperwork for a major order from a Chicago gift shop and for a bunch of individual orders. Then I worked on my accounts receivable until five o'clock, when Joe called and asked where I wanted to eat dinner.

"Why not at home?" I said.

"That would be fine, but the state police technician downloaded all the WinterFest records he could find from Mary Samson's computer—"

"Oh! I forgot!"

"Yeah. I volunteered the two of us to send out last-minute news releases on the choral concerts this weekend."

"You say the technician downloaded the information. Does that mean we won't be using Mary's computer?"

"No, they didn't want us out there at the crime scene, so the guy put it all on disk. Can we use your laptop?"

"It ought to be compatible. Maybe we should take ourselves over to the Warner Point office. The committee files are there, and we might need some other information."

It took me until seven o'clock to get caught up—my penalty for wasting time nosing into Mozelle's background. I met Joe at Warner Point. We ordered French dip sandwiches, which Jason assured us was the fastest thing on the menu to prepare, and took half an hour simply to talk before we started work. I reported what I'd discovered about Mozelle—or thought I'd discovered—that afternoon.

Joe wasn't any more impressed than Hogan had been.

"It doesn't matter, Lee. Even if you prove Mozelle knew Mendenhall, even if you prove she had an affair with him and that her mother got him fired—and what you found out is definitely not evidence—it still wouldn't matter. One, she was in Chicago, and two, Mendenhall didn't have her phone number. And if he had her phone number, he didn't call her."

He patted my hand. "You've got to get over this fixation on Mozelle."

"I guess you're right. In fact, I've probably got her whole psychology down wrong." I sketched the description of Mozelle's mother that Aunt Nettie had given me and the gossip I'd gotten from Johnny Owens.

"True, her mother sounds like the type to get a professor fired if he had an affair with her daughter," I said. "But the Mozelle we know would never have let her mother run her life that way."

"You're right. Even when Mozelle was young, she was probably as bossy as she is today." Joe looked at his watch. "It's eight o'clock. Are you ready to tackle Mary's files?"

I drank the last of my coffee. "Lead on."

Mary's files were incredibly well organized. As we'd expected, all her news releases were in one electronic folder, and they were dated to indicate which ones should be sent out when. And, yes, she'd already written the ones reminding the news media about the next week's activities, including the choral concerts. In her e-mail files, we found the addresses for the dozens of newspapers and television and radio stations she'd been sending the releases to.

Sending the releases wasn't a quick job. We had to read everything over carefully to make sure no last-minute changes needed to be made. By nine thirty we still hadn't actually gotten the e-mails on their way, and they'd have to go in batches.

Plus, Warner Pier didn't yet have high-speed Internet and e-mail access. We were working with slow, outdated dial-up.

"At this point, this is a one-person job," I said. "You can go on home, Joe."

"Nope. Warner Point hasn't been a good place for you recently. I don't want you out here alone."

"I'm not alone. There's a restaurant in operation here. Even if all the customers go home, Jason and his kitchen crew are in the building."

"Not this building. They're in a connecting building. I don't want you to be that far away from people."

I assured Joe I wasn't nervous, but he simply shrugged. "It won't take much longer. I'll stick around."

I didn't want to tell him I was grateful. But I was.

I kept working on sending the news releases by e-mail.

The second batch of news releases went to television stations, and Gordon Hitchcock's name headed the list.

And when I saw it, I knew—simply knew without question, as if I'd been hit by lightning—how Mendenhall had gotten Mozelle's phone number and how he could call it without having it show up on his cell phone records.

I was so excited I jumped up from the computer, sending my chair flying and startling Joe out of a stupor. Then I yelled at him, "Joe! He saw her on television!"

Chapter 20

Joe looked completely confused. He had no idea what I was talking about. So I explained.

"Yesterday Aunt Nettie and I retraced the actions we thought Mendenhall took after I dumped him at Motel Sleaze, and we did it at close to the same time of day he'd been dumped. To begin with, the desk clerk said Mendenhall had asked where he could get another bottle, and the clerk told him he'd have to cross the street and go to the supermarket.

"So that's what Aunt Nettie and I did. We waded through the slush over to that shopping center. And the first store we reached on the other side of the street is an appliance store. And it has ranks of television sets in the window."

Joe nodded. "Yeah, I know the place you mean."

"We went on to the supermarket, we looked at the liquor, and then we came back the same way. And as we passed that appliance store, that jerk Gordon Hitchcock was on all the television sets in the window, giving the news!"

Joe still looked blank, so I went on. "When Gordon Hitchcock came to the shop last week, he told me he'd run a long interview he did with Mozelle, and he said he'd rerun parts of it on Tuesday. And that's the night Mendenhall was killed."

Joe got it then. "We can check that on the tape Hitchcock gave us. And if he ran the interview then, Mendenhall could have seen Mozelle on television. But, Lee, would Mendenhall have recognized her? Even if he'd known her when she was in college, that was thirty years earlier."

"Mozelle's face is young looking, Joe. She just dresses conservatively. Her hair is the same color it's always been. If she and Mendenhall actually lived together . . . Well, I think he would have recognized her. He could have gone inside the store and found out her name. It probably ran across the bottom of the screen. Or he could have called the station. She's the only French in Warner Pier. It would be easy to get her phone number from Information."

"But he didn't use his cell phone to call her."

"No! Joe, he didn't have his cell phone with him. At the same time Mendenhall would have been walking over to the shopping center looking for booze, you would have been knocking on the door of his motel room. When he didn't answer, you phoned him."

"Right. I could hear the cell phone inside the room, but he didn't answer it."

"Mendenhall had gone out for booze, and he'd left his phone behind. Then he saw Mozelle on the television set. He listened long enough to get her name. He must have called her from a pay phone." I stopped, triumphant. "Has Hogan checked to see if Mozelle got any phone calls that evening?"

"Probably not, since he's been assuming that Mendenhall didn't have her number. And I'm sure nobody—not Hogan, not Alex VanDam, not McCullough—has checked calls made from pay phones in that shopping center."

Joe yanked his cell phone out. "I'll call Hogan."

"Not on that phone."

Joe scowled. "Oh, yeah. Warner Point is in the dead zone." He turned toward the regular phone. "I don't want to interrupt your computer. We need to get those news releases sent. I can run over to the restaurant; Jason will let me use his phone." He took a step toward the door, then paused. "But I don't want to leave you here alone."

"Go on! I'll be OK. I want Hogan to know about this."

"I'll lock the door behind myself. And I'll hurry."

After he left, I concentrated on calming my racing pulse. I sat down at the computer, trying to put my new brainstorm out of my mind long enough to work on sending the news releases. I had managed to send one more set—I was sending them to ten addresses at a time—when I heard a key in the door's lock.

"That was quick," I said, turning around to greet Joe.

But it wasn't Joe coming in the door.

It was Mozelle.

For a moment I was paralyzed. Mozelle. The person I was convinced had murdered two people. She was here. So was I. And I was the person who was trying to prove she was guilty.

It was just the two of us. At night. In a lonely part of a huge building.

Then I got hold of my nerves. Mozelle didn't know I'd "proved" how Mendenhall could have contacted her. She was probably simply dropping by because she needed something from the WinterFest files. It was only a casual encounter. Stay cool, I told myself.

Besides, Joe would be right back.

But I looked around the WinterFest office for some sort of weapon or shield. Something I could grab if Mozelle went berserk. I didn't see anything. What was I going to do, throw a file folder at her? Grab up my laptop and use it as a shield? Stab her with a freshly sharpened pencil? I eyed the desk lamp, remembered that Mendenhall had been beaten to death with a similar object, and shuddered.

Obviously guile was going to be more effective than violence. I smiled what I hoped was a harmless, innocent smile. "Hi, Mozelle. You're here late. Still working on WinterFest?"

"No, Lee, I came to talk to you."

"Oh, how did you know I'd be here?"

"Amos Hart heard from George, who had seen Joe, who had told him you'd be working on those releases out here tonight. Oh, you know, Lee, Warner Pier is a small town."

"That's true. Too true. So, Mozelle, what can I do for you?"

Mozelle's reaction to my question was stunning. She began to cry.

"Oh, Lee," she said, "have pity on me!"

The self-possessed Mozelle was in tears? And asking me to have pity? I couldn't believe it.

"Mozelle! What's the matter?"

"You've found out my secret." She was wringing her hands. "Please! Please don't humiliate me in front of my home community."

Humiliate her? I was thinking of sending her to prison, and she was afraid I might embarrass her? Mozelle was obviously thinking about something other than two murders.

I pointed to the chair Joe had been using. "Mozelle, sit down and tell me what on earth you're talking about."

Mozelle sat down weakly. "I've just come from a long session with Chief Jones. And, Lee, he wanted to know all about that episode when I was in college." She opened her purse and pulled out a nice white handkerchief—no shredded tissues for Mozelle. Then she went on.

"Chief Jones didn't tell me you were the one who figured out that I knew Professor Mendenhall, but I know you were."

"I didn't figure it out, Mozelle. I just saw that you'd gone to a college where Mendenhall had taught, and I wondered if you knew him there."

"I ran into Johnny Owens, and he said you were asking questions about those days. So I knew you suspected." She looked at me with eyes brimming with tears. "Lee, please don't tell anyone. That was the worst experience of my life."

Worse than murdering someone? I was confused, and it must have showed in my face.

Mozelle went on. "I was terribly in love with Fletcher Mendenhall. I'd never cared for anybody like that before. And I never have again. I was—besotted. When he asked me to—well, I was even willing to share him with another girl. I absolutely adored him."

She gave a sob. "Then my mother found out I wasn't living in the dorm. She came to Gerhard to find me. She had a fit. I understand now. I had broken every taboo she believed in.

"But I was willing to break them. I wanted to stay with Fletcher. I would have faced down the college, my mother, society itself—everything and everyone to be with him."

As I began to understand, I found myself feeling sorry for Mozelle. "How old were you, Mozelle? Twenty?"

"Nineteen! And Fletcher was my whole life."

She gave a racking sob before she spoke again. "And he turned his back on me!"

"Oh, no!"

"I was willing to bear anything for him, and he told me to get out. He threw me out—he threw both me and the other girl out—trying to save his stupid job!"

"What a jerk!"

"Everybody on campus knew. He just tossed both of us aside. People laughed when I walked by. I was publicly humiliated. I had to come home with my mother and listen to her lectures."

"Oh, Mozelle! That was a terrible experience for a young girl!" I wasn't being phony. It was an awful thing to happen to a nineteen-year-old girl. I patted Mozelle's hand. "I'm sorry that I asked Johnny about it. I'm sorry you had to tell Hogan about it."

"I should have gone to him and told him about it right away. I see now that he wouldn't have spread it around town. But I was so ashamed."

"I won't spread it around either, Mozelle. We're all allowed some youthful mistakes."

"Oh, Lee! I'd be so grateful! I nearly died of fright at that WinterFest meeting when George said Fletcher was coming to Warner Pier. I hated to leave the WinterFest committee in the lurch, but I had to get away, had to avoid meeting him."

She retired to her handkerchief again, and I tried to think about what she'd told me. If Mozelle had killed Mendenhall, it would certainly be understandable. But she wouldn't have had any reason to kill Mary Samson.

Maybe she hadn't killed either of them.

I spoke softly. "Mozelle, did Mendenhall call you?"

"No! Thank God! I would have died if I had heard his voice! I was so glad my name wasn't on that committee list, that George hadn't sent him my number."

She gasped out another sob. "I decided it was safe to leave my watercolor in the show, even though he was to judge it. I was working in oils in the days when I knew him, doing non-representational work. I felt sure he wouldn't recognize my new style. And he knew me as Marguerite, not Mozelle. Plus, Fletcher had no way to learn my married name."

"So he didn't call you."

"No! Even if he had called, I wasn't home. And I turned off the answering machine."

"Then you really did go to Chicago?"

Mozelle looked embarrassed. "Actually, no. But I left town. I called my Chicago friends, but they were going away. I couldn't stay with them. And I couldn't afford the Ritz-

Carlton this month. So I just went over to Kalamazoo and stayed at the Holiday Inn."

I swallowed a laugh, picturing Mozelle hiding out at the Holiday Inn, but telling all her friends she was at the Ritz-Carlton.

But wherever she had been, she'd destroyed my theory of who had killed Mendenhall.

If she'd had a long session with Hogan, and he'd asked her about her past, I was sure he'd checked out her whereabouts as well. He would know she'd been in Kalamazoo—if that was where she'd been. And he wasn't holding her. So he must think she was telling the truth.

I sighed. "I was sure Mendenhall had found out who you are now and had tried to call your house."

"If he did, he didn't get me, because I wasn't there. The only person who might have been at the house was Amos Hart. He promised to go by to feed my cat."

"What time would he have been there?"

"Probably before he went to chorus rehearsal. Between six and seven?"

Yikes! That was the time when I had guessed that Mendenhall might have called Mozelle's house. I frowned. Then I remembered that Mary Samson had been killed, too. Mozelle and Amos had given each other alibis for that.

"You and Amos were at his house after the art show opening, weren't you?"

Mozelle looked embarrassed. "Yes, that was the night— well, I hate to admit it, but I fell asleep. I had a glass of wine at the art show, and that always makes me sleepy. Then Amos simply insisted that I come by, have another glass of wine, and hear some new classical CD he had bought. At the time I thought my friendship with Amos might amount to something, so I was trying hard to take an interest. But—I'm just a musical nincompoop. Classical music puts me right to sleep.

I didn't wake up until nearly midnight. And Amos made a big thing out of it. You know, insinuating remarks. And he didn't want to give my house key back. He claimed he'd misplaced it. After that evening I decided our relationship must end."

I was staring at Mozelle in astonishment. My theory of her guilt was smashed, but she'd given me a new theory.

Amos. Amos Hart. Amos who believed that everything happened for the best. Amos, who could have been at Mozelle's house if Mendenhall called. Amos, who might have put a little something in Mozelle's wine so that she would sleep while he ran over to Mary Samson's house and beat her head in with a skillet.

Amos, who at that moment opened the door to the office and walked in. Holding a pistol.

Chapter 21

"Amos!"

"Amos?"

Mozelle and I spoke at the same time, but with different inflections. She was surprised to see Amos, but wasn't disturbed by him, even though he was carrying a pistol. I was scared out of my gourd.

Amos might have had a pistol, but he wasn't pointing it at us when he came in. He was pointing it toward the floor.

"Yes, it's Amos," he said. "Good old dumb Amos. Good for picking up the tab. Good for being an escort. But not good enough to be a permanent companion."

He raised the pistol and pointed it at Mozelle.

She seemed finally to realize we were being threatened. At least she took a deep breath then, and I didn't hear her let it out.

Amos kept talking. "I was good enough to try to protect your reputation when that creep Mendenhall called and threatened to slander you. I was good enough to drive nearly to Grand Rapids, good enough to shut his lousy mouth forever. Good enough to spend hours trying to protect you."

Amos paused as if he were waiting for a reply. I didn't

have one, but Mozelle spoke. She still sounded more mystified than scared.

"All I asked you to do," she said, "was feed my cat."

Amos laughed harshly. "Amos the cat feeder. Amos the useful vote on the committee. Amos who helpfully answered the phone, thinking it might be an important call. Amos who's going to take care of you permanently—and take care of this nosy Lee Woodyard. And her husband."

Joe! Joe was going to come back from using Jason's phone any minute. And he was going to walk in on this scene with no suspicion that something was wrong. And I had no way to warn him.

Or did I? Moving slowly, I stuck my hand in my pocket.

"Don't move!" Amos' harsh bark was a long way from the tone of his beautiful tenor solos.

I yanked my hand out of the pocket and held it up.

"Keep your hands on the desk," he said. "And you, Mozelle, you keep your hands still, too."

"Why?" Mozelle said. "Amos, why are you doing this?"

"You're not as smart as you pretend to be, are you? Don't you get it? You told me yourself that the police suspect you of killing Mendenhall and Mary Samson." He waved the pistol, but he kept it pointed in our direction. "I found this little gun in your bedside table. I guess your dear late husband—the one you never mention—had it. You're going to kill Lee and Joe with it. Then, dear lady, you're going to commit suicide, out of remorse."

"Amos," I said, "no one will believe that."

"Oh, yes, they will. With no one around to remember my mistakes."

"What mistakes?"

"The snowstorm! You're famous for your slips of the tongue. I guess it's contagious! You were the very person I talked to about driving to Grand Rapids in a snowstorm. And the only night it's snowed in the past two weeks was the night Mendenhall was killed. And the chocolate snowmen! I thought they were all over town. But, no! Only Mendenhall had a box of the stupid snowmen until the day after the art show opening. They were in his room! Pretty soon you were going to figure out where I saw them."

"I didn't even think about either of those things."

"But you would have! Besides, who knows what Mary Samson told you! And you and your handsome, brilliant husband would have blabbed to your uncle, the police chief. So you've got to go! I'm just sorry I didn't get you the first time I tried."

It did cross my mind that I wasn't going to die not knowing who killed Mary Samson. At least that question was answered. But I wasn't ready to die at all.

Far away, across the building and out in the restaurant parking lot, I could hear a horn honking, the sound caused by the panic button of a car. Would it only mislead Joe? Would he run into the parking lot, instead of back to the WinterFest office? Were there still diners in the restaurant? Would he think the racket came from someone else's car?

As I stared at Amos Hart and worried about Joe, the answer to my questions came. The door behind Amos moved, just slightly.

Someone was there.

It simply had to be Joe.

I exhaled, and my breath trembled, almost becoming a moan. Joe had come. I had punched the panic button on my car keys, and the sound had alerted him. Or else he had simply come back from making his phone call and noticed the door he'd left locked was now ajar.

But I realized the light was out in the long corridor leading to the office. I felt sure Joe was outside the door. But he couldn't simply walk in and grab Amos. He needed to surprise him.

I would have to distract Amos.

"Amos!" My voice was loud. "Why Mary? Why did you have to kill her? She was so harmless."

"Harmless! She talked to Mendenhall! God knows what he told her! And she asked you to call her so she could discuss it with you. I had to shut her up before the two of you put your heads together."

The door moved another inch. I had to keep Amos' attention focused on me. "Then I guess you drugged Mozelle so you'd have an alibi."

Amos sneered openly. "The only drug Mozelle needs is a glass of wine and a classical CD. She pretends to be cultured, but she can't listen to classical music without falling asleep."

Now a hand was reaching in the door. I recognized the cuff. It was the cuff of the plaid wool shirt Joe was wearing. He was reaching for the light switch, the switch for the overhead light.

"I guess you gave Mozelle extra wine at the reception."

Amos laughed harshly. "She's too polite to pour it in the potted plant."

I slowly moved my hand across my laptop. Where was the button on the desk lamp?

Everything seemed to happen at once.

Joe hit the switch for the overhead light. He yelled, "Get down!"

I punched the switch on the desk lamp. The room went dark. I yelled, too. "Get down, Mozelle!"

Two figures were struggling. I jumped up, and went toward them. A shot banged out, echoing against the room's hard walls.

Someone screamed, a high bone-chilling keen.

People were scrambling around on the floor. I tried to get to the door. I ran into someone. We both fell down, and we scrambled around, too.

"I've got the gun!" That was Joe. "Turn on the light!"

Somebody had hold of my ankle, and I couldn't get up. I started crawling toward the door, toward the light switch, but these hands kept hauling me back.

I yelled, "Let go!" But the hands kept their grip.

The door was outlined by a dim light, probably a reflection from lights back at the entrance to Warner Point. Now it became larger, and I realized it was the silhouette of someone leaving the room.

"Let go!" I kicked at the hands holding my ankle. "He's getting away!"

Another figure rushed past. I saw Joe's shape briefly as he went out the door.

If Joe had run out, I deduced, he must have been chasing Amos. So Mozelle was the person who had hold of my ankle.

"Mozelle! Let go of my ankle!"

She let go, and I was on my feet. I ran down the hall, back toward the main building of Warner Point. As I ran, I yelled, "Catch him! Stop him!" Anything to get attention, to keep Amos Hart from getting away.

Suddenly I was in the entry hall, with the art show rooms on my left, the restaurant on my right, and the main entrance door straight ahead. Jason was advancing from the restaurant, clutching a huge cleaver. And Joe had beaten Amos Hart to the main door.

Amos danced from side to side. Joe was between him and the door. Jason was coming at him through the restaurant, and two waiters and a dishwasher were behind him. Mozelle and I were running toward him down the long hall from the WinterFest office.

Amos ran into the art show.

Joe followed and grabbed at him. Amos slithered away. One of the temporary partitions went down with a crash. Amos crashed with it. He got up and again tried to run. This time he went headlong into Johnny Owens' giant metal reindeer. The reindeer toppled. For a moment I thought Amos was going to be impaled on its aluminum horns.

We all yelled, "Look out!" But Amos was falling, out of control. He landed in a tangle of antlers, tail, and hooves. This time he didn't get up. He wasn't hurt, but he was pinned down by the heavy sculpture.

In the silence, Mozelle spoke. "I do have the worst taste in men."

I hope never to have another evening like that one. But at least we now understood what had happened.

Amos Hart, dropping by Mozelle's house to feed her cat on the Tuesday night Mendenhall arrived, had answered her telephone. It had been Mendenhall, wanting to talk to the woman he had once lived with in a threesome with another young girl. In his drunken state he had poured out the secret Mozelle had kept for thirty years and had hidden in the Kalamazoo Holiday Inn to preserve. Amos was shocked. He may have thought he was hearing a scandalous lie. He determined to see Mendenhall face-to-face and convince him not to repeat his story.

Amos went on to his rehearsal, sent the chorus into sectional rehearsals, then quietly left the church and drove to Lake Knapp. If anyone missed him, they merely thought he was in with a different set of singers.

When Amos talked to Mendenhall at the motel, it became clear that he would not be able to shut up the former professor. So Amos beat him to death with the desk lamp.

In a side note, Hogan later got a call from Sergeant McCullough. He had followed up on Aunt Nettie's conviction that Mendenhall might have asked for a visit from a call girl. She had been right, McCullough admitted. When he tracked the girl down, she said she went to Mendenhall's room and knocked, but no one answered. She left, but as she was getting into her car, she saw a tall man come out of the room. She didn't get a good look at him, but his overcoat had been hanging open, and she could see that he was wearing a bow tie.

Aha!

At the WinterFest committee meeting the day after he killed Mendenhall, Amos had learned that the art show juror had talked to Mary Samson. From her embarrassment he deduced that Mendenhall had made off-color remarks. Amos feared they had been about Mozelle.

Mary hadn't seemed sure just what Mendenhall had been saying. But Amos was afraid she would figure it out, especially when he learned Mary was planning to talk to me about it.

To give himself an alibi, he lured Mozelle to his house and plied her with two things he knew would make her sleep: wine and classical music. Then he went to Mary's house and murdered her.

With a good attorney, Amos might make a case for manslaughter or second-degree murder in the death of Mendenhall, but poor Mary's killing was first-degree murder. There was no other way to look at it.

Amos later maintained that he had done all this—plus defacing the art show catalogs—to protect Mozelle.

But Mozelle had caught on to Amos. First she had figured out he was mainly interested in her because he thought she was comfortable financially. Second, she had begun to understand the self-righteous creepiness of his personality. In the scene I overheard, she had given him the door.

One other mystery was explained three days before Christmas, when Aunt Nettie came into my office, closed the door, and sat down with a serious look on her face.

"Lee, I'm going to ask you to do something that you're not going to want to do. Something you're going to think is immoral, and that I know is illegal."

I looked at her warily. "You don't want me to put preservatives in the chocolate, do you?"

"Good heavens, no! I'd never do that."

"Then what?"

"Sarajane's 'friend' needs a job for a little while. Off the books."

"Off the books? We can't do that!"

"Sarajane and George have authorized me to explain who the 'guest' is, Lee. Then you'll understand why we have to do this."

It seemed that Sarajane, formerly an abused wife, and George, a member of the board of the Holland woman's shelter, had become involved in that secret movement that is sometimes whispered about, but that most people deny exists. In cases when its organizers believe the only safety for an abused woman lies in a new identity, she is spirited across the country though a modern-day "underground railway." The women are handed from person to person, with no single "conductor" knowing where they will wind up.

"George says they make the exchanges in the Wal-Mart parking lot," Aunt Nettie said.

"That's an ideal spot. It's always crowded, and people are moving sacks and packages from shopping carts to cars. Who's to notice a little extra activity? But why did both Sarajane and George go to Wal-Mart on the same evening?"

"George was picking up the lady who's now staying with Sarajane, and Sarajane was sending a previous 'guest' on her way. The woman currently staying with Sarajane is named Sharon. She needs to earn some money."

I sighed. "I can put her on the books as contract labor and hope she doesn't earn enough to get us in trouble."

"She'll be here only briefly, Lee. No more than a month."

"It seems to me that law enforcement isn't too supportive of this system of sanctuary. What does Hogan think?"

"He and I are careful not to discuss it." Aunt Nettie smiled her sunny smile. She came around the desk and gave me a hug.

"Thank you, Lee. And happy holidays."

"Happy holidays to you, Aunt Nettie."

One other effect of the whole case, according to the Warner Pier grapevine, was that Reverend Chuck Pinkney preached a heck of a Christmas sermon. It wasn't his usual "believe and all will be forgiven" theology. God's people might be forgiven, he told his congregation, but that didn't give them license to continue sinning. It meant they had to try to reach a higher standard. And while God could produce good out of evil, that was no excuse for doing the evil. And anybody, he said, who thought particular beliefs or virtues or good works were going to produce worldly rewards had better think again.

I didn't hear the sermon, but I did give some serious thought to my own failings and sins. I told Joe as much on Christmas Eve.

"I'm thoroughly ashamed of the way I judged Mozelle," I said.

"Oh, I don't know that you were too harsh on her. She is a genuine, unmitigated pain in the neck."

"Yes, but now that I understand why, I'll try to be more patient."

"So you think her early experience with Mendenhall warped her personality?"

"Her experience with Mendenhall and her mother's reaction. When Mozelle kicked over the traces at nineteen, two disasters followed. Her mother declared her ruined for life because she had defied society. Then Mendenhall didn't even value the sacrifice she had made for him. He just threw her aside."

"That would mark anybody's personality."

"Mozelle must have lived her entire adult life too frightened to be anything but conventional ever again. She could never relax and just do what she wanted. She had to be publicly virtuous." I raised my hand to swearing position. "I hereby resolve to try to be nicer to her."

"You'll get to test your resolve tomorrow, since I understand she accepted Aunt Nettie's invitation to Christmas dinner."

"Yep. It will be a grand multifamily occasion." Aunt Nettie had invited Joe's mom; her boyfriend, Mayor Mike Herrera; my friend Lindy, with her husband and three kids; Joe and me; and now Mozelle. Plus Aunt Nettie and Hogan.

"It's going to be a big day," I said. "So we'd better get on with our private celebration tonight."

"Do you need me to help bring in that giant item you tried to hide under a tarp on the screened-in porch?"

"You saw it!"

"It's hard to miss something that big, even in the dark."

"Well, I've been careful not to ask about that huge thing in the basement."

"Let's start with the porch item. I'm curiouser than you are."

The porch item was an easy chair and ottoman in a fabric and style that blended with the new couch that was our official gift to each other.

Joe immediately tried it out. "It's great," he said, "as long as I still get to sit on the couch with you now and then."

"You'd better! And the chair didn't come out of the family budget. I bought it with the money Jason paid me to set up his bookkeeping system on his new computer—and to teach him how to use it. Now, you bring that big thing up from the basement."

The basement item wasn't very thick, but it was more than two feet from top to bottom and more than three feet from side to side. I could feel a raised edge through the wrapping paper.

"It must be a great big tea tray," I said.

"Just open it."

Inside was a framed print of Bob VanWinkle-Snow's spectacular view of a storm over Lake Michigan.

Tears came to my eyes. "Joe! I love it! It's fabulous."

I resolved not to say a word about how much it must have cost. Bob's work was way out of our budget.

Joe put his arm around me. "And now I can pay off the Visa bill."

"Huh?"

"Bob and Ramona needed some shelving and storage cabinets in their darkroom. I bought the materials—the stuff you found on my Visa—and they paid me back yesterday. I got the photograph in exchange for building the cupboards and shelves."

"Oh, Joe! I'm thrilled!"

"It's part of a limited edition of prints. The best-of-show photograph was number one. This is number nine."

We hung it over the mantelpiece, replacing a sentimental print of flowers that my grandmother had hung there forty years earlier. It looks beautiful.

Everybody brought something to the multifamily Christmas dinner. My contribution was turkey and Texas-style corn bread dressing. I love Michigan food, but dressing has got to be made with corn bread.

Aunt Nettie baked a ham, and Mike Herrera did a pork loin. The two of them are already arguing over who gets to play host for next year's Christmas dinner.

Moral Chocolatiers

Many of England's early chocolate manufacturers, it happens, were Quakers. Joseph Fry & Sons, Cadbury's, and Rountree were all prominent in the business during the early part of the nineteenth century.

Following the social consciousness principles of their faith, the Quaker industrialists made efforts to set up ideal living conditions for their employees, and both Cadbury and Rountree established model factory towns for their employees. Interestingly, American chocolate maker Milton Hershey—who was not a Quaker—did this in the United States, founding the town of Hershey, Pennsylvania.

The Fry family became concerned about deplorable conditions for workers on cacao plantations in Portuguese West Africa and boycotted cacao from that area. This has been echoed in the early twenty-first century with the Fair Trade movement that strives to ensure a fair profit for growers of coffee and cacao in emerging nations.